AF492748

SEAGRASS SECRETS

SALTWATER COWBOYS, BOOK 4

CHRISTY BARRITT

Copyright © 2020 by Christy Barritt

All rights reserved.

No part of this book may be reproduced in any form or by any electronic or mechanical means, including information storage and retrieval systems, without written permission from the author, except for the use of brief quotations in a book review.

CHAPTER ONE

FIREFIGHTER COLBY MORRIS pulled the protective gear over his head as sideways rain and blowing sand pelted him.

In all his years living on Cape Corral, he couldn't remember the last time a downpour had been this driving. He now understood why people had termed the phrase "buckets of rain." That was exactly how this storm felt.

The whole island was drenched, and no relief was in sight. According to forecasters, this weather system would stick around for at least two more days.

"Morris, are you there?" Fire Chief Dillon McGrath's voice crackled over the radio.

Colby pulled the device from his belt and raised it to his mouth. "I'm here, Chief."

"Any sign of our caller?"

Colby continued across the dark, secluded property. The Currituck Sound stretched in the distance and an oversized barn—a social barn, as Colby liked to call it—stood behind him.

Colby had ventured away from that area and paced toward the woods instead.

"Nothing out here except a lot of water," Colby muttered into the radio. "Even the wild horses knew to find shelter tonight."

"They have better instincts than most people."

"True that."

About an hour ago, dispatch received a call from an injured man on the outskirts of town, not far from what locals called Smith's Hope. The land was owned by Smith Cooper, but he let the community use the one-hundred-acre property for celebrations and get-togethers.

Apparently, a man had been trespassing here tonight when he'd fallen and broken his leg. Colby and Dillon had come to find him. However, the man's call had kept breaking up, making it hard to understand him.

As Colby slogged forward, pitch-black air

surrounded him, every inch of it seeming to retain the moist atmosphere. It was so wet outside that Colby might as well be swimming.

On a good day, it would be difficult to find someone on this isolated stretch of land. Tonight? It felt downright impossible.

"Keep looking," Dillon said. "I recruited Levi and Dash to help also."

"Roger that." Colby put his radio back on his belt and pushed forward.

His boots slopped through the oversized puddles saturating the sandy ground. The rain had nowhere to go, so instead, the water pooled on the surface.

Based on the information the man had given, Colby and Dillon had pinpointed the most probable area where the caller was located. The man's phone had apparently died, so they couldn't call him back to check on him.

Colby continued sloshing through the area, the beam of his flashlight bouncing through the rain-tattered air.

Just up ahead, a small shed appeared near the edge of the woods. The structure looked old—probably fifty years at least and perhaps left over from a previous owner.

Maybe their caller had taken shelter inside.

Colby started toward it. As he reached a small overhang on the south side of the building, the beam of his flashlight caught something.

Was that a footprint?

Colby knew the mark had to be fresh. Otherwise, runoff from the rain would have washed it away.

His heart rate quickened.

He grabbed his radio and gave Dillon the update.

"Keep searching," the chief said. "I'll head that way."

"On it." Colby followed the steps around the side of the building, knowing as soon as he stepped from beneath the overhang he'd probably lose the trail.

The footprints seemed to lead toward the woods in the distance.

Had the man collapsed somewhere in the boggy wilderness?

The impressions in the sand looked surprisingly normal—not what Colby might expect from someone who'd broken his leg. In that case, he'd anticipate drag marks.

Tension pinched his back muscles.

"Hello?" he called over the wind and rain.

Nothing.

He wanted to find this man and then finish the game of Settlers of Catan he'd started with his friend

Emmy Sutherland earlier this evening. Colby had clearly been about to win when he'd gotten called into the station. He wanted to see the look on Emmy's face when he announced victory once he established the final settlement on the game board.

But that would have to wait.

Pulling his hood down again, Colby walked deeper into the woods.

As he stepped behind an oversized oak, something came down on his head.

Before he realized what was happening, pain radiated from his skull.

The next instant, everything went black.

***

"THIS WHOLE ISLAND is going to sink!" Emmy Sutherland said through clenched teeth as she stared out her truck windshield.

Her hands gripped the steering wheel as a torrential downpour flooded everything around her. Making matters even more complicated was the inky-black sky and the wind gusts that stirred up not only the rain but also sand.

Her visibility was at zero.

Even though Emmy was well familiar with the

terrain, she still took the drive slowly. The last thing she needed was for one of the island's wild horses to dart out in front of her.

In other circumstances, she might even worry about a person running across the road. But no one in their right mind would be out in this weather.

Except Emmy.

She frowned.

Ordinarily, she wouldn't go out on a night like this. But a friend from church—Lily Ann—just had a baby and had run out of diapers. Since Lily Ann's military husband was out to sea, Lily Ann had called Emmy. Emmy had then managed to convince the owner of the town's general store to stay open past normal business hours to let her buy some supplies for her friend.

With her good deed done and baby Jonas now dry and happy, Emmy headed home.

The windshield wipers rushed back and forth in front of her, but the metal arms were unable to keep up with the steady stream of water pouring from the sky.

The nor'easter seemed to attack the island today like a monster rising from the sea. The storm pushed the ocean up on the shores, making the road running alongside the beach nearly impassable.

Instead, Emmy traveled on an interior road cutting through her island home. But the water still puddled in low-lying areas, sometimes as deep as two to three feet.

Two to three feet was enough to stall out her dad's old hand-me-down Dodge truck.

She leaned toward the windshield as more water cascaded from the sky. She felt like she was driving through a waterfall. In pitch blackness. Blindfolded.

"Maybe I should just get out of the truck and walk." She leaned even closer to the windshield, desperate to see.

But she knew walking would be a bad idea also. She just needed to be more patient.

As the road pitched downward, Emmy squinted, trying to see just how deep the water might be at the base of the hill.

Either way, she couldn't slow too much or she wouldn't make it back up the incline on the other side.

Swallowing hard, she pressed the accelerator.

As she did, her tires collided with the water at the base of the hill. The wheels churned a moment before finding traction again.

Emmy pressed the accelerator harder, afraid water might get to her engine and ruin the motor.

The puddles hadn't only been formed by the fresh rain—they were also partially filled with saltwater from the ocean. Saltwater and metal weren't a good match.

Just as she started to speed, her truck lurched to a stop as a loud thump sounded.

Emmy hit the brakes and froze, hardly able to breathe.

What had just happened?

As a blast of rain seemed to hold its breath, her headlights illuminated something in front of her.

Not a dog. Please not a dog. Or a horse.

Emmy didn't think that was what she'd hit.

Actually, it was worse.

Emmy couldn't be certain, but she was pretty sure she'd just hit a person.

CHAPTER TWO

"COLBY? COLBY? ARE YOU OKAY?"

Colby groaned and tried to sit up. What had just happened?

He reached for his head—which throbbed uncontrollably.

As his eyes opened, he glanced around.

A dark, watery wilderness surrounded him.

Then the memories hit him.

As he'd been looking for the injured man who'd called 911, something had slammed into his head.

Fire Chief Dillon McGrath stared at him now, flashlight in hand. Colby squinted, his head pounding harder, and motioned for his friend to lower his beam.

"Are you okay?" Dillon knelt beside him, obvious concern on his normally stoic face.

Colby nodded but let out another groan. "I think so. I was looking for the man when someone hit me over the head, and I blacked out."

Even in the dim light, Colby saw the fire chief grimace.

"I'll take you to the clinic to be checked out, just in case." Dillon had to yell over the pouring rain.

Colby waved him off, ignoring the throbbing in his head. "I'll be okay for a few more minutes. Did you find our guy?"

Dillon shook his head, the lines around his eyes tightening. "No, I didn't. I'm going to scan this area one more time. He's got to be around here somewhere."

Colby let out a breath and started to stand. As he did, Dillon stretched out his hand to help him up. Colby blinked the rain from his eyes as he tried to find his balance.

Dillon's flashlight scanned the ground. More footsteps marred the soil. But the prints showed signs of a scuffle.

Were these left by the man who'd knocked Colby out?

That was Colby's best guess.

Silently, Dillon and Colby followed the tracks deeper into the woods.

As they reached a small clearing, Dillon's flashlight illuminated something. Two shoes appeared on the murky, moist ground ahead of them.

Shoes that were attached to legs.

Legs that belonged to a man's body.

Dillon rushed to the figure and put two fingers to the man's neck.

When he looked back up at him, Colby knew the truth.

This man was dead.

Colby shone his flashlight on the man's chest.

A bullet hole gaped there.

WITH TREMBLING HANDS, Emmy grabbed the door handle. As soon as she pulled the lever, the torrential rain slithered inside the opening and battered her.

She ignored the soaking downpour and plunged herself outside.

Emmy rushed toward the front of her vehicle, both desperate to see what she'd done and dreading it.

Her headlights barely illuminated the water-laden air.

The area right in front of her truck appeared empty—except for a massive puddle.

As Emmy cleared the edge of the vehicle, she gasped.

It was just like she feared—a man sprawled in front of her bumper.

"Oh, no!" Emmy knelt on the wet ground beside him. "Are you okay?"

The man groaned.

He was alive. That was good news, at least.

But what kind of damage had Emmy done to him? Did she really want to know? How had this even happened?

"I called for help," she murmured. "Paramedics are on their way. Just hang in with me."

The man groaned again.

Emmy pushed wet strands of hair from her face as she looked down at the man. She needed to keep him lucid. If he fell into an unconscious state, she feared he wouldn't awake.

As the man's head fell back to the ground, water surrounded him, nearly reaching his eyes. She'd learned enough first aid from Colby to know she shouldn't move an accident victim in case he had a spinal injury, but she couldn't sit there and let him drown.

Moving quickly, Emmy leveraged the man's shoulders onto her lap before the puddle and blowing water covered his face.

"What's your name?" Emmy gripped his hand, occasionally squeezing it to keep him awake.

"Jeremy," he managed to say, his lips barely moving and his voice raspy with pain.

"Hi, Jeremy. I'm Emmy. I was driving the truck. I didn't see you. I'm so sorry."

The man grabbed his side and moaned again.

The darkness and rain made it hard to see, but Emmy barely made out dark hair and the start of a beard. The man appeared to be around her age, but he definitely wasn't from around here. Emmy could tell by his khaki pants and polo shirt.

People here on Cape Corral didn't, in general, dress like that. The island was home to working-class folks more prone to wear cowboy boots and hats than loafers.

"You've got to . . . help me . . ." The man's voice came out as a croak.

Emmy squeezed his hand, desperate to offer some type of comfort as he suffered. "The best thing you can do right now is to be still. Don't move. Help should be here any minute now."

His eyes opened and latched onto hers.

Emmy saw something there. Pain? Fear?

She knew this was all her fault.

How had she let this happen?

Thankfully, just then, she saw flashing lights in the distance.

Help was here.

Emmy prayed Colby was in that vehicle.

Seeing him always made everything better.

But she knew he'd been called to a different emergency this evening.

Besides, was there any possibility this situation could be anything but terrible?

CHAPTER THREE

COLBY SLUMPED as he sat on the edge of the bed in the emergency triage area at the Cape Corral Medical Clinic.

The small building was located at the south end of the narrow island and was only designed to accommodate about four patients at a time. A temporary treatment area had also been set up near the waiting room for people like Colby—who only needed a quick check by the medical staff.

One doctor worked there, and he only came to the island three days a week. Otherwise, the clinic was staffed with two nurses and several assistants. Thankfully, Dr. Knightly was there today.

Dillon had insisted Colby be checked out, even though Colby knew he was fine.

He really wanted to be out on the scene with their dead body. He wanted to know what was going on.

But that wasn't his job.

Colby's job was to rescue people. But tonight, he'd needed rescuing.

Go figure. He tried not to be proud, but his ego was a little bruised.

In the meantime, Levi Sutherland—Emmy's brother—and Grant Matthews were on the rescue-turned-recovery scene. The two men, along with Dash Fulton, served as law enforcement here on the island. Dillon had left for another call, taking a few volunteer firefighters with him.

It was a busy night here in Cape Corral.

"How are you doing in here?" A nurse he instantly recognized threw open the curtain to his treatment area, her overly cheerful voice grating on his nerves.

"I'll be better when I can leave."

Jocelyn giggled as she stepped closer to examine the cut on his head. "Soon enough, Colby Morris. Soon enough. You just don't worry about anything. I'll take good care of you." She pursed her lips before tapping his nose and handing over a cold compress. "This will help with the swelling."

Colby swallowed hard. He and Jocelyn had been on a couple of dates, but he wasn't interested in taking their relationship further. The woman was pretty enough with her bouncy blonde hair and wide smile.

But that special "it" factor just wasn't there.

Jocelyn hadn't seemed to get the memo.

He frowned and held the compress to his head, wishing he could have a do-over.

As Jocelyn began talking about her plans for Christmas, Colby couldn't get the image of the dead man out of his mind.

Someone had shot him.

Here on Cape Corral.

Things like that weren't supposed to happen in their town. The island had eight thousand acres that were mostly undeveloped, making it perfect for the wild horses who'd made their homes here. On one side, the ocean rumbled strong and mighty. On the other side, the Currituck Sound rolled peacefully, acting as a nursery for sea life.

There was no place like Cape Corral.

Yet these kinds of crimes seemed to be happening more and more often lately. Maybe it had something to do with the fact that the one and only bridge leading to the town had been washed out in the summer. Crews should start rebuilding it any time now. Until then, the only access to the island was via boat or, for a lucky few, helicopter.

As Colby heard a commotion in the distance, he peered out, anxious to know what was going on.

He spotted a man being wheeled inside on a stretcher. Dillon walked beside him.

And following on the other side was . . . Emmy?

Beautiful Emmy . . . her slender figure soaked to the bone, her porcelain skin muddy and wet, her normally luscious dark hair now stringy with moisture, and her long limbs visibly quaking.

When Colby's mom had left him, and his father had turned to drinking, Emmy had been there for Colby. She'd taught him how to shoot a bow and arrow. Had checked on him to make sure he did his homework every night. Had offered him hugs when he'd felt all alone in the world.

They'd bonded ever since then.

Concern filled him now.

What was Emmy doing at the clinic?

Had she been hurt?

Colby's lungs froze at the thought of it. He quickly excused himself from Jocelyn and hopped off the exam table.

He had to know what had happened to his best friend.

EMMY SPOTTED Colby in the distance, and relief filled her. Something about his broad frame, tousled blond hair, and easy-going manner always made her feel better.

He seemed to spot her at the same time and strode from the curtained-off triage area toward her. His eyes narrowed with concern as he studied her.

"Emmy? What happened? Are you okay?"

As soon as Colby reached her, Emmy threw her arms around him. She knew she must look frightful, with her soppy wet clothes and tangled hair, but she didn't care.

Colby had seen her at her best and at her worst. They'd been best friends since second grade and were thicker than thieves, as her mom used to say. There was hardly a night that Emmy went to bed without talking to Colby first—and she never wanted that to change.

"Oh, Colby . . . I hit someone."

He stiffened in her arms. "Hit someone? What do you mean?"

Emmy pulled away and wiped beneath her eyes using the sleeve of her black sweatshirt. "I was driving back from Lily Ann's place. It was so dark, and I could hardly see anything. The next thing I knew, my truck lurched to a stop. I didn't even see anyone outside. I don't know where this man came from."

Colby's eyes trailed the stretcher as it disappeared into one of the rooms down the hallway. "Is the man okay?"

"I . . . I think. I mean, I talked to him a little."

"Did you recognize him?"

"No, I didn't. He's not a local." Emmy buried her face in her hands. "Oh, Colby . . . what if he dies? It will be all my fault."

He pulled her into his arms again and held her. But the embrace only lasted a moment when a realization hit Emmy.

Colby was being treated here at the clinic also, wasn't he? He'd just come from a room . . . and he had a bracelet on his wrist.

Emmy stepped back and studied him. His motions were stiff, a cut stretched across his forehead, and he looked like he'd taken a late-night swim—in the swamp.

"What happened to you?" she asked. "You look horrible."

He chuckled—but only for a second—before running a hand over his face. "It's a long story, but I'm fine now. Dillon insisted I come here to be checked out, just as a precaution."

"Oh, Colby." Emmy touched his cheek, worry washing through her. "Are you sure you're okay?"

"I'm sure. I've been through worse . . . like when you and I participated in that pig wrestling competition in front of the whole town."

She smiled. "Why was that bad for you? I was the one whose jeans ripped—on camera."

Colby chuckled. "I gave you my flannel shirt so you could tie it around your waist."

"And I appreciated it. At least my humiliation was for a good cause—raising money for the food bank."

"And it gave people in town something to talk about."

Before they could chat anymore, Fire Chief McGrath stepped into the waiting area and walked toward Colby.

"We have a problem," he muttered.

Emmy tensed as she waited for what he would say.

"More overwash is coming in from the ocean," Dillon said. "The water's starting to flood the clinic. I need your help."

CHAPTER FOUR

AN HOUR LATER, Colby, Dillon, and several volunteer firefighters had secured sandbags near all the clinic doors to slow the spread of water inside. Emmy, despite her shaken state, had pitched in to help.

That was one more thing to love about her—she was never afraid to get dirty. She also realized the importance of the clinic to the area. They couldn't risk the building being compromised.

She disappeared forty minutes into the job so she could give her statement to Dash, another law enforcement officer on the island.

When Colby finished filling the last sandbag, he wiped his brow.

He and Dillon stepped inside while a couple other members of the crew offered to clean up.

Colby drew in a deep breath as he glanced across the waiting area. "What now?"

Dillon stared at the doors at the entrance, his jaw hard. "Now we keep an eye on things. There's not much else we can do."

"I've never known this clinic to flood, and I've lived on this island my whole life."

"Between the high tide, the full moon, and the storm sitting off the coast, forecasters are expecting higher than usual flooding for this area. I just never envisioned this."

Colby shook his head, wishing the combination wasn't making life so difficult for everyone here on the island. "I always wondered why this clinic wasn't built on stilts like everything else here on the island."

"Probably because it was built inland. Up until now, it's never been a problem."

Colby couldn't argue with that statement. "Do you have any idea how many patients are here right now?"

"Just one," Dillon said. "The man we brought in tonight who was involved with the auto collision."

Colby's gut clenched. The collision that *Emmy* had been involved with.

Seeing her so upset had done something to Colby's heart. If only he could take all her problems and worries away, to make things better for her.

Just like Emmy always did for everyone else.

He knew that wasn't possible, though.

Dillon remained where he was, his gaze still glued on the entry doors as if he expected to see water flooding inside at any minute. "How's Emmy holding up?"

Colby frowned. "She's pretty shaken. You don't think she'll be charged with something, do you?"

"It's doubtful," Dillon said. "Law enforcement will have the final word, but the collision was truly an accident."

"What about the dead body we found in the woods?"

"Levi's out there right now, working against the elements to try to collect any evidence he can find."

Colby crossed his arms. "Did you recognize the man?"

"I didn't. He isn't a local."

That's what Colby had thought also. "I don't know what's going on here on this island."

"I would like to know who hit you over the head." Dillon glanced at him, his gaze darkening.

"My guess?" Colby said. "The killer."

"You're probably right." Dillon's frown deepened. "I'm glad you're okay. All things considered, it could have been worse."

"Yes, it could have been." Colby shifted. "Listen, if it's okay, I'd like to go check on Emmy."

"Of course. But I want you to take the rest of the evening off. You need to take care of yourself after that injury today."

"But—"

"No buts about it. I'll call you if I need you. Otherwise, take it easy."

Finally, Colby nodded, knowing better than to argue with Dillon. "Got it, boss."

Part of him was relieved—because part of him wanted to check on Emmy without fear of being called away again. Though she hadn't said it, Colby sensed that Emmy needed him. That's just the way things had always been between them. They were there for each other.

As he took a step down the hallway so he could find her, his phone rang.

It was Levi.

"Colby." Levi's voice sounded tight and clipped. "Where's Emmy?"

"She's here at the clinic."

"I heard about the collision," Levi said. "Look, I need you to keep an eye on her for me."

"What do you mean?"

"The dead man we found this evening? Emmy's address was in his pocket. Until we know why, we need to assume it wasn't because he was looking for a place to stay."

Concern welled in Colby.

Against all odds, the night had just turned even worse.

"I don't like the sound of that," Colby muttered. "Does Emmy know?"

"Not yet. Do you want to mention it to her?"

"I can do that."

"Great. I'll check in later."

Just as Colby ended the call, someone yelled his name down the hallway. Dillon.

Colby looked up at him. "Yes?"

"The sandbags are breaching," Dillon said. "We need your help."

"MR. RIESLING SAID it's okay if you'd like to speak with him," Dr. Knightly told Emmy as she lingered in the hallway.

Emmy's heart thumped in her chest as she pushed from against the wall. She offered the doctor a stiff nod before stepping toward the man's room.

Part of her didn't want to face the music, as the saying went. She'd rather bury her head and pretend like none of this had happened. The whole thing still seemed like such a nightmare.

Clearing her throat, Emmy pushed a long hair behind her ear and stared at the man's room. *Mr. Riesling's* room.

She could do this.

She knocked lightly before hearing a "Come in!" from the other side.

Pushing the door open, Emmy stepped into the room and saw the man she'd hit laying on the hospital bed. An IV dripped beside him. Several stitches stretched across his forehead. But otherwise, he seemed okay—all things considered.

Emmy studied the man for a moment.

He was handsome with dark hair and a neat beard and mustache. He appeared to be fit and was probably five or six years older than Emmy was, if she had to guess.

What a welcome he'd had to this island.

"Hi there." Emmy swallowed hard, guilt flooding through her.

A tired smile pulled across one side of the man's lips before a weak, "Hey" escaped.

She stepped closer, her lungs tightening until it was hard to breathe. "I'm Emmy."

"I remember. I'm Jeremy."

"How are you doing?"

He shrugged. "I'm still alive."

Emmy nodded at his midsection. "Any broken ribs?"

"Only bruised. All in all, I'm okay. I have a slight concussion, a cut on the side of my leg, and some stitches on my face. I'd say I could be much worse."

"I am *so* sorry." Emmy rubbed her throat as it started to clench. "I promise, I was looking at the road. But it was so dark and rainy, and I didn't see—"

He raised a hand to stop her. "It's okay. I had no business being out at night. I should have seen your headlights."

Emmy tilted her head ever so slightly. "If you don't mind me asking, where did you come from? It was like you appeared out of thin air."

He let out a long breath. "The house where I was staying . . . the wind took part of the roof off. I've never seen anything like it. I went to get in my truck, but the ground was flooded all around it—like, really flooded. I didn't know what to do, so I went looking for help. I got discombobulated, and it was so hard to see. I really don't know what I was thinking—only that I needed help."

"Then you just happened to run out in front of my truck?" Emmy frowned as she tried to picture it.

"I was going to flag you down. But I lost my footing. The ground was wet, and it was so dark and . . . I'm not even really sure how it happened. The next thing I knew, I was in front of the truck, and I felt it hit me."

She cringed at his words. "Again, I apologize. I feel terrible."

"You have nothing to feel terrible about. Let's just say it's been a bad evening for both of us."

"Let me pay your hospital bill, at least." Emmy's money was tight right now, but it was the least she could do. This man shouldn't have to fork out money for this.

"I would never ask you to do that . . ."

"I insist."

Just as the thought rushed through her head, she heard the wind blowing outside. Sand blasted the building and more sheets of rain seemed to hammer the roof.

This weather was insane.

A knock sounded on the door behind her, and Dr. Knightly stepped inside. His face looked grimmer than it had earlier. "I have bad news."

Oh, no . . . *more* bad news? What else could possibly happen tonight?

"We're going to have to evacuate the clinic," Knightly continued. "Unfortunately, we can't keep the flood waters out, which means that it's not safe to stay here."

Emmy's mind raced. This man's rental home had been compromised. Where else would he go in his injured state?

There was only one place that made sense to her.

Emmy had four extra rooms at the inn.

Jeremy could stay in one of those.

That, along with paying his medical bills, would help her feel a little better about all this.

Now she needed to convince Jeremy of that.

She wasn't going to take no for an answer.

<h1 style="text-align:center">CHAPTER FIVE</h1>

COLBY SET his pen on the table.

He'd just spent the last thirty minutes filling out an incident report at the clinic.

Now he wanted to check on Emmy.

He couldn't get that note out of his head—the one with Emmy's address on it.

Why would that man have Emmy's house number? What sense did it make? He needed to talk to Dillon and get to the bottom of this.

As Colby walked down the corridor toward the waiting room to find Dillon, he spotted Emmy stepping out of a room, her arm around someone Colby had never seen. She and Nurse Jocelyn helped the man into a wheelchair.

Colby tensed as he watched the scene. That was

the man Emmy had hit, wasn't it? Colby didn't have to be at the accident to know that.

But why was Emmy helping him now?

"Colby," someone called.

He turned to see Dillon jogging his way.

"Thanks for all your hard work." Dillon paused in front of him. "But we're going to have to evacuate the clinic. The sandbags aren't working—which is what I feared. We need to get our accident victim out of here and then try to save as much of this equipment as we can."

Alarm rushed through him. That didn't sound good. "What do you need me to do?"

"Could you give Emmy and our accident victim a ride back to the inn?"

Colby's muscles clenched as he let Dillon's words sink in. "A ride back to the inn? Both of them?"

"That's right. Emmy said Mr. Riesling could stay there for the evening. He can't stay at the clinic, and his house was damaged in the storm."

"I see." But Colby's words sounded tighter than he'd intended.

Dillon exchanged a look with him and it seemed like he wanted to say more. Thankfully, Emmy and Jeremy caught up with them just then.

"I heard you're going to give us a ride back,"

Emmy said as she walked alongside the man in the wheelchair. Jocelyn pushed the man toward the exit.

Colby shoved aside the quick spark of protectiveness he'd felt—a spark he couldn't fully explain. "I'll get you guys back to the inn and out of this place."

Emmy smiled. "You're the best. Oh, by the way, Jeremy, this is my best friend, Colby. Colby, this is Jeremy Riesling."

The two of them nodded at each other.

Instantly, Colby didn't like the man. Or was it that he didn't trust him? After all, that dead man had a note with Emmy's address in his pocket.

What if someone on this island had ill intentions toward Emmy?

The first people Levi and his guys would look at would be visitors.

Colby's concern had nothing to do with the fact that this guy had his arm around Emmy moments ago.

Or did it?

Colby swallowed hard, trying to keep a hold of his emotions.

Because he'd never told anybody this.

But he had been in love with Emmy since the second grade.

And telling her that was a risk he couldn't take.

EMMY SAT between Colby and Jeremy on the bench seat of Colby's pickup truck.

Rain still pounded everything in its path, the darkness seemed even darker, and the wind rocked the vehicle back and forth. Colby skirted the edges of puddles, making for a rough ride.

Even though Emmy had lived here since she was born, tonight's driving conditions still got her heart racing. She stood by her earlier comments that no one should be out in this.

"So, where are you here visiting from?" Colby asked Jeremy, his hands tight on the steering wheel.

"New Hampshire."

"And what brings you down to Cape Corral?" Colby continued.

Emmy noted that Colby seemed more uptight than normal. Was it everything that had happened tonight?

Most likely.

There had been some crazy things unfolding on the island lately, but tonight just might take the cake. She couldn't blame her normally laid-back best friend for being slightly on edge.

"I'm actually a screenwriter, and I came here to find some inspiration," Jeremy said.

"A screenwriter?" Emmy asked, instantly intrigued.

"That's right. I haven't sold anything yet, but I'm getting closer."

"Well, hopefully your story is full of storms and intrigue," Colby said. "Because, if it is, you're going to find a lot of inspiration here in Cape Corral right now."

Jeremy chuckled. "I gathered that. I do apologize that you're having to go out of your way to help me right now."

"Oh, he doesn't mind," Emmy said. "Do you, Colby?"

"Of course not." But Colby's voice sounded stiffer than usual.

Finally, they pulled up to Emmy's inn.

The old farmhouse was located right beside the Community Safety building where the police and firefighters were stationed. Behind the building was the stable where the horses used to patrol the island were kept.

At first, Emmy hadn't liked the more modern building being built so close to her space. But, over time, she'd come to appreciate being so close to the guys. It was one of the reasons Colby and her brother Levi could stop by so often. Plus, if she ever had trouble, they were right next door.

On the porch, Emmy fumbled with her keys for a moment—thankful that she even *had* her keys—finally flinging the door open. Before running inside herself, she ushered Jeremy in.

To her surprise, Colby stepped inside also. Emmy had figured he would try to rush right back to work.

"This is a nice place." Jeremy glanced around. "I appreciate you letting me stay here."

The scent of popcorn still lingered in the air, and the game she and Colby had been playing sat unfinished on the table. Several popcorn kernels were on the floor where she and Colby had an impromptu food fight.

That wasn't to mention the Christmas tree that had been set up in the corner. She and Colby had decorated it this past weekend. Stockings hung on the mantel, and a miniature Christmas tree centerpiece sat on one side of her farm-style kitchen table.

She had more decorating to do, but Christmas was still a few weeks away, so she had some time.

Only a couple of hours ago, things had felt so normal. And now . . .

She turned back to her guest and plastered on a smile.

"I'm glad you can stay here. This is what we do here on the island. We look after each other. Now, let me show you to your room. I'm sure you're anxious to get cleaned up and get some shuteye."

Colby shifted beside her. "If it's okay, I'll wait down here for you."

"Of course."

Emmy wasn't used to her friend sounding so serious. Colby was the kind of guy who liked to taunt her with garter snakes and to jump out to scare her when she was least expecting it.

Emmy looked back at Jeremy. "Come on. Your room is right up here."

She'd get her guest settled . . . then she was curious to hear what Colby had to say.

Because he obviously had something on his mind.

COLBY SWALLOWED HARD when he saw Emmy coming back down the stairs several minutes later.

She looked tired. But beautiful. She *always* looked beautiful.

Emmy had a natural kind of good looks. She didn't need makeup, her hair looked good however she fixed it, and her figure was slim—even though she never watched anything she ate.

In Colby's eyes, she was pretty much the perfect woman.

She paused in front of him and glanced up, curiosity in her eyes. "What's up? Are you okay?"

Colby's hands went to his hips as he offered a stiff nod. "I'm fine. It's you I'm worried about."

Emmy pointed at herself. "Me? Why are you worried about me?"

Colby nodded up the wooden staircase. "Because you're letting this man stay at your house. Alone."

She cocked her head to the side, as if trying to follow his line of thought. "Colby, I let strangers stay at my place all the time. I run an *inn*."

He let out a sigh, trying to find the right words to explain himself. "This is different."

"How is it different?" Emmy raised her chin, challenging him with her gaze.

That was okay—Colby could handle a debate with her. The two of them had always been honest with each other—except when it came to Colby admitting his feelings for her, at least.

"For starters, there's no one else here," Colby stated.

"This isn't a first. There have been times in the past when I only had one guest." She crossed her arms. "What else do you have?"

"Secondly, it's storming outside, and it's going to be harder for you to get in and out—or for help to get here if you need it."

Emmy cocked an eyebrow. "Is that all you've got? I expected more from you, Colby."

"Thirdly, what if this guy needs medical help? What are you going to do then? You don't even have a truck here."

"He *is* going to need assistance while he's here. The reason he needs assistance? Me." She pointed to herself. "Because *I* hit *him* with my truck. If he needs something other than what I can provide, I'll be calling either you or Dillon. Anything else?" Emmy tapped her foot, amusement dancing in her gaze.

Colby opened his mouth but closed it again. Finally, he gave what he thought was his most compelling argument. "You shouldn't be going in and out of his bedroom."

Emmy's eyebrows shot up. "How else am I going to take care of him?"

Colby shrugged, knowing that his argument was

futile right now. Despite that, he couldn't seem to stop himself. "Maybe he can stay on the couch instead."

"Colby . . ." Emmy stared at him, her lips puckering as if she held back a smile.

He could see the thoughts racing through her mind and waited for what she'd say next.

"Remember that time when you had the flu last year?" she continued.

Colby nodded, knowing exactly where this was going. He braced himself for her argument.

"You stayed here at the inn, and I took care of you," Emmy continued. "I was in and out of your room as well."

His jaw hardened. "That was different."

"Why?"

"Because it was me."

Emmy let out a laugh and laid her hand on his chest. "Colby . . . why are you so wound up tonight? What's going on?"

He tried to relax his shoulders. Maybe he was overthinking this. "Maybe it's just my head injury."

Some of the irritation in Emmy's eyes turned into concern. "Do you have to get back to work?"

He shook his head. "Dillon told me to take the

night off, that he'd call me if he absolutely needs me."

"Then that's what you should do. You should take the night off." Emmy nodded as if the decision was made.

"But the clinic is flooding and—"

"And I'm sure that Dillon, Levi, Dash, and all the volunteers are going to help do everything they can to save it," Emmy assured him. "You need to take it easy after what happened. In fact, speaking of the couch, why don't you just take it easy here for a while? It's already the middle of the night, and the weather outside is atrocious. You'd be better off just resting at my place."

"I don't want to impose." Even as Colby said the words, he couldn't stop thinking about what a great idea that would be on more than one level.

What if the killer knew Emmy's address? It was a possibility. They still didn't know why that information had been in the dead man's pocket. Until they knew, everyone should be on guard.

Either way, Colby wanted nothing more than to keep an eye on this stranger in Emmy's house. He didn't know what it was about the man, but Colby didn't trust him. His gut told him to be cautious.

"You've never cared about imposing before."

Emmy gave him one of her looks, one that made him feel giddy inside.

Colby shrugged. "But it's really only fun to impose on you if it bothers you."

She grinned. "Then consider me bothered."

His expression quickly sobered. "There's something else I need to tell you."

"What's that?"

How did he even say this? "The dead man we found tonight . . . your address was in his pocket."

CHAPTER SIX

EMMY COULDN'T GET Colby's words out of her mind. She wanted to believe there was a good, harmless reason that man had her address. But she hadn't been expecting any guests here.

And the man had been murdered.

The thought made her feel jumpy.

She tried to compose herself as she stood in Jeremy's room. She'd already delivered some clean towels, water bottles, and a bag of toiletries to the man. Since he'd come here with nothing, Emmy was trying to make sure he had everything he needed.

Colby still waited for her downstairs, and Emmy craved the safety that came with being near her best friend.

"You sure do think of everything." Jeremy twisted the top of the water bottle.

Something about seeing him smile caused a surprising rush of flutters in Emmy's stomach.

Why was that? The reaction didn't make any sense to her.

Emmy *loved* being single. She had no desire to date or to even get married one day. As she liked to tell people, she loved being wild and free.

Not wild in the sense of a person without boundaries. But wild like the horses here on the island whose only limitations were the water surrounding the island.

To Emmy, that seemed like the perfect life. It also ensured she never got her heart broken again—like she had with Derek Jenner. Emmy had to admit there were times it would be nice to have someone else help her carry her burdens—like right now, as money at the inn was tight.

But she was making out just fine . . . most days, at least.

She cleared her throat, pushing those thoughts aside, as she turned her attention to the present. "If you need me, you have my cell phone number. Even though I'll be at the house, it's the best way to get in touch with me. I'll keep the phone close."

Jeremy held up his cell. "Thankfully, my phone wasn't ruined in the accident. Maybe tomorrow I can pick up a charging cable from my rental."

"I can check to see if I have a spare one here."

"You always go the extra mile, don't you? Thank you again for everything. You've been a real lifesaver."

Emmy frowned. She didn't know about that.

With one last look at her guest, Emmy shut the door and went downstairs.

When she reached the first floor, she spotted Colby sitting on the couch, his feet propped up on her coffee table, and a bottle of water in his hands.

She just couldn't understand his grumpiness today. It wasn't like him. He was fun-loving, playful, and warm.

She sat down beside him. Now that Jeremy had turned in for the night, Colby had all of her attention. Emmy looked up at him now, studying his face.

He looked tired and worried. His eyes—which were normally dancing and mischievous—looked dull. His tousled hair didn't look as much carefree as it did unkempt.

"I can't believe somebody hit you," she murmured.

Colby rubbed the top of his head and frowned, almost as if embarrassed. "Me neither."

"Whoever did this to you just came out of nowhere?" Emmy tried to picture what happened.

Colby shrugged. "I was out by Smith's Hope, looking for someone who called and needed a paramedic. This guy—the killer—must have been hiding in the shadows when I walked by."

Emmy pulled a buffalo-check pillow into her lap and frowned. "What about the dead body? I just can't believe you found a dead man."

"Neither can I." Colby ran a hand over his face. "I'm still trying to process everything."

"Well, I'm glad that you're here now. Do you want me to get you some coffee? Hot chocolate? A slice of my cherry pie? I know you can't resist my cherry pie . . ."

That got a small smile out of him. "Now that you mention it, some hot chocolate and pie really does sound great."

"One hot chocolate with pie coming up then."

Emmy slipped into her kitchen. If there was one thing she loved, it was hospitality. She usually cooked for her friends at least once or twice a week, not to mention the guests who stayed at the inn. Something about having sweet and savory aromas wafting through her house made her feel surpris-ingly whole and fulfilled.

Running this inn was what Emmy was meant to do. She felt like she was made for this kind of work. She only wished finances weren't such a struggle right now.

Just as she came back into the living room, thunder clapped outside. She flinched, and the liquid almost spilled over the edges of the white ceramic mug.

"Thunder? In December?" she questioned. "Like the rain hasn't been bad enough."

"Tell me about it."

"I feel like the storm is never going to end." She lowered herself beside Colby again.

"If by never you mean not for the next two days, then you'd be correct." Colby picked up the hot chocolate and took a sip. "You make the best hot chocolate. Have I ever told you that?"

"I think you just like to eat and drink whenever you can. Kind of like a teenage boy."

Colby chuckled. "I can't deny that. But it's only because you make everything so tasty."

"Whipped cream?" She held up a can.

"Yes, please."

Instead of putting it on the pie, Emmy squirted

some on the tip of Colby's nose and grinned. "Wait, you didn't mean you wanted it on your dessert, did you?"

"Oh no, you didn't!" Colby took the can from her and made a beard on her chin amidst her squeals and laughter.

"No fair! You're stronger than I am!"

"No one said life was fair, Em."

She laughed again as Colby put the can down. As she stared up at her friend, their gazes caught and Emmy felt her heart thumping hard.

Thumping hard? Why in the world was it doing that?

It was almost like . . . like she was attracted to Colby.

The thought was ridiculous. He was practically like a brother to her.

Exhaustion from tonight must be playing with her thoughts.

She quickly looked away. As she did, she wiped some of the cream from her chin and took a bite. "At least it tastes good."

"You look awfully cute dressed as an edible Santa."

"Maybe you should try looking like an edible Santa. Maybe Jocelyn would like it."

His laughter faded. "Jocelyn and I just went on a couple of dates—nothing serious."

"It's never serious with you, is it?"

He shrugged. "She's a nice girl, but we were just missing that spark, you know?"

"Did you tell her that you didn't want to see her again?"

"I didn't ask her out again. Doesn't that count?"

Emmy shook her head. "Oh, sweet boy. To be a man and so naïve to the ways of women . . ."

He shrugged again. "I don't know what you want me to say. I didn't make any promises."

Breaking women's hearts seemed to be a common theme with Colby. But Emmy had already given him a hard time about it before. Tonight had already been long, so she'd save any additional aggravating for later.

Just as Colby was about to take a bite of his pie, his phone rang.

Emmy froze as he answered.

As she listened to the one-sided conversation, she sensed that something else was wrong.

Colby put the phone away and stood. "It looks like I won't be taking it easy here tonight after all."

"What's going on?" Concern rushed through her.

Was it the clinic? Or had something happened to one of the island's wild horses?

"They think that lightning struck one of the buildings up on the North Banks. We've got to get the fire out."

The North Banks? That was where the notorious Ferguson family had bought numerous properties—and they were trying to buy more. The purchases and their plans for the land were a point of contention on the island.

"It happened at Thomas Ferguson's house," Colby said, almost as if reading her thoughts.

A sick feeling roiled in Emmy's gut.

This wasn't good . . . on so many levels.

IT TOOK two hours to put the fire out.

The flames licked the backside of the structure, near the laundry room. Thanks to the rain, the blaze hadn't spread quickly. Other than some superficial damage and smoke, the home seemed otherwise okay.

Right now, the smell of soot hung in the air, mixing with the aroma of rain. Early morning sunlight was beginning to break on the horizon.

It had been a long, long night.

"Colby, come in here," Dillon called.

Colby sauntered across the floor, his gear weighing his body down by at least forty-five pounds, and paused in front of Dillon. "What's going on?"

"I want you to look around this room and tell me what you see."

Colby knew that Dillon was just looking out for him, trying to make him a better firefighter by teaching him the ropes. Colby had just been hired full-time about a month ago. Until then, he'd been an EMT and a volunteer.

But Colby hated to be tested.

Mostly because his father had done the same thing to him.

It had never turned out well when he did. It had mostly ended in fights and Colby being pushed around in one of his father's drunken rages.

Colby glanced around the room, studying the charring patterns along the walls to determine the source of origin. The lowest and deepest point of burning usually indicated where the fire began.

Colby's gaze stopped at something in the corner.

Realization spread through Colby as he examined the area more closely.

Was he seeing what he thought he was?

He swallowed hard before finally saying, "This wasn't started by lightning at all, was it?"

Dillon said nothing.

"There are two points of origin for the fire." Colby glanced at Dillon. "That can only lead me to conclude that this was . . . arson."

Dillon nodded stiffly. "My thoughts too."

"But who would have set a fire at Thomas Ferguson's house?"

Dillon's gaze locked with his. "That's what we're going to need to figure out. We're going to need to call the county investigator so he can help."

EMMY WAITED UP ALMOST all night for a call from Colby about the fire.

She'd heard nothing.

Instead, she kept thinking about that note with her address. She hadn't been expecting anyone at the inn, so a potential reservation shouldn't be the reason for it.

But if not that, then what?

The fact that the man had been murdered didn't comfort her. In fact, every time the wind hit her house or thunder cracked outside, Emmy had nearly jumped out of her bed.

The sun was now slowly rising in the sky, though gray clouds waited just offshore like an army waiting for orders to attack.

Most likely, since Emmy hadn't heard any bad news, that meant everyone on the scene of the fire was okay. News spread fast here on the island.

Still, Emmy would be preoccupied until she heard a confirmation. She'd been cooking all morning—homemade waffles with baked peaches. The house smelled heavenly as the scent lingered in the air.

Emmy carried a tray loaded with waffles, orange juice, and fresh fruit up to Jeremy's room. She was the reason this man was in this state, so she wanted to do everything she could to help him feel better.

Emmy paused at his door and drew in a deep breath before knocking.

A lazy sounding, "Come in" came from the other side.

Emmy plastered on a smile as she twisted the handle and nudged the door open.

"Good morning." She held up the tray in her hands. "I have breakfast."

"You didn't have to do that." Jeremy sat up in bed, looking more bright eyed than she'd thought he would.

That had to be a good sign.

"I like this kind of service," he murmured.

"I wasn't sure if you'd be too sore to make it

downstairs, so I decided to bring breakfast to you." She set the tray in his lap. "How are you feeling today?"

"I can definitely feel that something happened to me, but overall, I'd say I'm doing fine."

"That's great to hear." Emmy pointed to the tray. "I didn't bring coffee because I didn't know what you took in it."

"Just a little bit of cream would be great. But you don't have to go downstairs now. Sit and talk for a while."

After hesitating a moment, Emmy lowered herself on the end of the bed.

She didn't say anything for a moment, simply let her guest eat in peace. He seemed to especially like the waffles and baked peaches on top of them.

"You're a great cook." Jeremy paused with a forkful of pastry in the air.

Emmy felt her cheeks heating. "Thank you. I enjoy it."

"Tell me, how long have you owned this place?" He slowed down between bites as he listened.

She glanced around at the clean, wood-paneled walls that had been painted white. At the wrought-iron bed frame. At the cozy accessories that made this house feel like home.

"This used to be my grandfather's place," Emmy started. "When he passed away four years ago, he handed it down to me, and I opened this inn. The rest, as they say, is history."

"I'm sorry for your loss. But I have to say, you really seem like a natural with decorating and hospitality."

Emmy shrugged, even though she secretly delighted in his compliment. "I enjoy it and get to meet a lot of interesting people."

"I'm glad you had room for me."

She waved a hand in the air. "Lucky for you, this is a slow time of year."

It was one of the reasons money was tight. On top of it being a slow season, Emmy had some unexpected repairs pop up that had set her back financially. But she knew it would all work out.

Hopefully.

"It's not unusual for businesses to shut down this time of the year around here, is it? When I was looking on the rental sites, it seemed like most vacation companies didn't take reservations from after Thanksgiving until March."

"That's the way it used to be around here. That schedule is starting to loosen up a bit more as the need becomes greater." Emmy shifted, wondering about the man in front of her. "You must have come here for the wild horses. You want to use them in your screenplay, don't you?"

He paused with his glass of orange juice in the air before nodding. "How'd you know?"

"That's usually everyone's reason for coming here—that or fishing, and you don't strike me as the type who wants to write a fishing story."

Before they could talk anymore, the front door creaked open downstairs.

Her shoulder stiffened.

Who was here?

What if it was the person who'd killed the man last night?

And what if Emmy was for some reason next on his list?

COLBY TRIED NOT to bristle when he saw Emmy come down from Jeremy's room. He still hadn't identified exactly why he had this reaction to the man. Was it because Emmy's eyes lingered on her new guest a little too long?

"Colby?" Concern stretched through her voice.

"The one and only." He narrowed his eyes. "Why do you look so worried?"

"I guess I just have a lot on my mind."

"Did something else happen?"

She waved a hand in the air. "No, nothing. I'm just on edge." She grinned at him. "In other news, it's good to see you."

When he saw the smile stretch across her face, all of Colby's troubles seemed to disappear like fog in the sunlight. "You too."

"How's everything going?"

Colby ran a hand over his face, trying to figure out how to answer that question. He was going on twenty-four hours with no sleep, he had a raging headache, and he was worried about Emmy.

"I'm tired but fine," he finally settled on saying.

A spattering of rain hit the window just then, causing Emmy to jump again.

She wasn't usually this jumpy. But maybe everything that had happened was playing on her emotions more than she wanted to admit.

Besides, this weather just wouldn't let up—nor would the tension on the island.

"What happened with the fire?" Emmy frowned as her gaze turned to him. "I've been waiting to hear."

"It looks like arson."

"What?" Disbelief whispered through her voice.

Colby nodded stiffly. "It's true. Someone set it on purpose."

"That's terrible. You have no idea who?"

"Not yet. Dillon is with the county fire investigator now, but he said cases like this can be hard to resolve—especially if there are no witnesses."

"That's too bad." Emmy shook her head and stared off in the distance. "I wonder if the fire is somehow connected with the dead body."

Colby shrugged. "I haven't seen any connection that would indicate that. But . . . ?"

"Either way, it seems like a good day to hang out inside and stay away from anything and everybody."

"Maybe." He shifted. "I wanted to let you know that we had your truck towed back to the station. There's a slight dent in the bumper, but it's still drivable. I fiddled with a few things under the hood, just to make sure everything was safe."

"I love it when you look out for me. Thank you."

Colby frowned. "There is one thing you should know . . ."

Emmy tilted her head, a knot of confusion forming between her eyes. "What's that?"

"We left your truck at the site last night—we

couldn't get Lloyd's Towing out. When we went back to get it this morning, we discovered that someone rifled through the interior. Everything was torn out of your glove compartment, and the papers under the sun visor were taken down."

EMMY GASPED at Colby's words. "What? Was anything damaged?"

"Not that we can tell."

"Stolen?"

Colby shrugged. "You'd know better than we would. I can't see where anything you keep in there would be valuable."

Emmy shook her head. "It wasn't. It's just . . . unnerving to have someone go through your things, you know? Especially considering everything going on right now."

"I know." Colby squeezed her arm, a tender look in his gaze.

Emmy swallowed hard, trying not to get sucked

into the warm depths of Colby's blue-green eyes. He had this way of looking at her that made her feel like he could see into her soul.

She'd never experienced that with anyone else.

She cleared her throat, pushing away those thoughts. "Does my truck somehow tie in with that note that was found with my address on it?"

Colby shrugged. "I wish I could tell you, but it's hard to say for sure."

Emmy frowned again. "I suppose you're right."

"At least you weren't hurt last night. That's the good news."

"I only wish Jeremy wasn't either . . ." Even though the accident was purely an accident, she couldn't shake the guilt she felt.

Colby glanced up the stairway at the mention of Jeremy. "How's your guest doing?"

Emmy shrugged and followed his gaze. "I guess he's okay. I don't anticipate him going anywhere anytime soon."

"Why's that?"

"No car, no house, no mobility—or limited mobility, at least. Need I go on?"

"I guess not. Sounds like I need to get used to the man being here—for a while, at least."

Emmy stared up at Colby, trying to read between the lines of his tone. There was no use. She had too much on her mind.

Instead, she asked, "Can I get you some coffee? Something to eat?"

Colby smiled. "There's not a single person who's walked in this house that you don't offer to feed, is there?"

"What can I say? It's my love language."

"It's just one more thing to love about you. You're always first in line to help when people need someone."

"Now you're just trying to make me blush, aren't you?"

His eyes sparkled. "Making you blush is awfully fun. I wish I could stay and do it for longer, but I have to head back to work."

A frown tugged at her lips. "No rest for the weary, huh?"

"No, not right now. Too much going on."

He took a step back.

Emmy didn't want him to leave. She wanted things to feel normal. She wanted to play Settlers of Catan or to toss a football or binge watch *Longmire* together.

But maybe another time . . . after all this craziness had passed.

COLBY TOOK a step away when Emmy called to him again.

"Before you go, how's the clinic?" she asked.

He paused. "I just heard an update before I came here. It has about six inches of water inside. They were able to move most of the equipment, so that's good news."

She glanced beyond him at the window. "It looks like it stopped raining for a minute. Speaking of which . . . I need to feed the cats. You want to come?"

"I have a few more minutes." A colony of feral cats lived in the woods behind Emmy's place. She gave them food and water every day.

It was just one more thing to love about her.

She grabbed a bag as he walked outside beside her.

"I heard heavy rain is supposed to start up again later," Emmy said.

"It is. The town is already pretty flooded. A lot of people's houses took on water. Some people's cars flooded while they were in the driveway even. What we need is some continuous sunshine to dry things up."

"That's terrible." Emmy frowned as she poured some kitty kibble into some bowls she kept at the edge of her property. "If there's anything I can do . . ."

"We'll let you know." Colby watched as several cats popped out of the brush at the sound of the food hitting the plastic bowl. Somehow, those cats seemed to weather whatever was thrown their way. They didn't seem any worse for the wear, even after the nor'easter had been sitting on the coast for days on end.

When Emmy finished feeding them, she turned toward him. "All done."

Colby hesitated another moment, in no hurry to leave her here. But he had no other choice. Dillon was waiting for him back at the station.

"I need to run, but I'll catch up with you later," he said. "If the rain ever clears, maybe we could toss around the football in the backyard."

Football and bonfires were his favorite ways to unwind. But really, anything with Emmy did the trick.

She smiled. "That sounds like just what the doctor ordered. But, until we have some drier days, dinner for sure. Tonight. Six o'clock."

A grin spread across Colby's face. Dinner with Emmy *did* sound like just what the doctor ordered. "That sounds perfect. I'll see you then."

Besides, it would give him a chance to keep an eye on Emmy . . . something that seemed especially important considering everything that was going on here on the island.

CHAPTER NINE

I'M GOING to find you!

His gut told him Luther was here on this island.

His gut was hardly ever wrong.

It was only a matter of time until he located the man.

His hands fisted at his sides with anticipation.

He couldn't wait to get his hands on the man. To *really* get his hands on him. To make him pay for everything he'd done.

Who did Luther think he was? Did he really think he could escape unharmed and without consequences?

Because Luther had another thing coming for him.

I'm not afraid to kill.

In fact, he'd done it last night.

His back muscles tightened as he remembered the satisfaction he'd felt when he saw his victim sink to the ground. When he'd seen the terror in his eyes. When he'd seen the last touch of light disappear from the man's eyes.

He wouldn't mind seeing that again.

He'd had just enough time to grab the man's phone, but it hadn't helped. There was nothing on it that helped him find what he wanted.

For now, he would blend in. It was the best way to find out the information he needed—information about Luther and his true reasons for being here.

No one was going to stop him from taking what was rightfully his.

He'd like to see someone try.

In fact, he could use more practice at extinguishing life, at watching the very soul of a person disappear from the physical body.

There was no greater honor—or duty—than acting as judge, jury, and executioner.

CHAPTER TEN

COLBY PAUSED beside Grant Matthews in front of the house where Jeremy Riesling had been staying. Sure enough, the roof had blown off and the man's truck was surrounded by water.

"What a storm," Grant muttered. "It might as well have been a hurricane with all the damage it's caused."

"You can say that again."

"Let's go check this place out. It's clear our victim won't be coming back here."

"You talk to the management company?"

"I did. They confirmed that Jeremy Riesling was staying here. He's from New Hampshire, thirty years old, and he appears to check out."

For some reason, that update disappointed

Colby. He'd been hoping that his gut was correct and there was something suspicious about the man.

"Let's get this done." Grant nodded toward the house.

The county building inspector would most likely condemn the house. In the meantime, Colby and Grant would pick up a few things to take back to Jeremy. There was no way the man could go back inside this structure—not if it put him in danger.

Colby and Grant had been tasked with this job this morning. Meanwhile, Levi was out talking to people and trying to identify their dead body. Dillon was talking to the fire inspector, as well as looking for witnesses and checking to see about any unusual purchases of various types of accelerants. Dash was helping with both, as well as checking on the island's wild horses.

"I'm surprised we haven't been able to ID our victim yet," Colby said as they climbed the steps into the rental house.

"No, we don't have a name for the victim," Grant said. "He didn't have a wallet on him, and no one has ID'd him yet."

"What about his phone? The man did call 911."

"I thought of that also, but it was gone—nowhere

to be found. Good Lord willing and if the creek don't rise, we'll find something on this guy."

Colby wanted to groan at Grant's antiquated verbiage. But he had too many other things on his mind.

Had the killer taken the man's phone? Colby's throat tightened.

If so, that showed that the person who'd done this was even more calculating than Colby had first assumed.

Colby glanced around the waterlogged house. After the roof came off, the rain had just poured inside. The good news was that the roof had only come off half the house.

An inspector for the owner's insurance agency would have to come to assess the damage later.

"What about those footprints I saw right before someone hit me over the head?" Colby asked.

"They were gone by the time we got to you. But don't worry. We'll keep looking for more evidence. That's what Levi is doing out there now. After this, I'm going to go patrol the island and check on some of our horses. Life goes on, right?"

Colby stepped into a bedroom and saw the items left there. This part of the house was the dry side.

"You want to grab some of his things?" Grant asked.

"Sure thing." Colby found the man's suitcase and threw some clothes from the dresser into it. He also grabbed a laptop and placed it in a bag by the desk.

There was nothing suspicious here.

Part of Colby wanted to dig through the laptop and bags—but he didn't.

That would be crossing the line.

When they were done, Colby and Grant left the items with Emmy and went back to the station.

Just as they stepped inside, Colby spotted a slight man with wire-framed glasses sitting in the reception area.

"Can we help you?" Colby asked.

"I hope so." The man lifted his briefcase into his lap. "My name is Gilbert Davies, and I'm with the East Coast Conservation Alliance. I'm here to monitor the island's wildlife for any signs of endangered species."

Colby felt a leap of excitement in his chest. Perfect.

They'd called this man in an effort to preserve land and stop it from being developed. The Fergusons were determined to build a resort in the area, and locals were determined to stop them.

The man was finally here. They'd called him nearly a month ago, but there was a wait-list before he could arrive.

"I'm so glad you could come." Grant stepped toward him. "I was just about to patrol the island. How about if you come with me? I'll give you a tour before the rain starts up again, and you can ask any questions you might have."

"That sounds great."

Just as the two walked away, Colby noticed the shadow at the end of the hallway. He looked to see who'd entered the building.

His stomach sank when he saw the familiar figure.

His dad.

What was he doing here?

A FEW HOURS LATER, Jeremy came downstairs dressed in some clothes Colby had dropped by earlier. His outfit wasn't as tailored as Emmy had thought it might be. Maybe that was a good thing considering his injuries.

The rain had stopped for a moment, even though the clouds still looked pregnant. Emmy had spent some time catching up on laundry and dishes while her guest rested upstairs.

"You made it down," Emmy said. "Is everything okay?"

Jeremy nodded. "Everything is fine. I'm thinking about stepping outside and getting some fresh air before the rain starts again."

Emmy put the laundry basket on the couch. "That sounds like a great idea."

He paused and leaned against the doorway, his hands dangling in his pockets and a casual look about him. "Any chance you'd like to join me?"

Emmy almost said no but changed her mind. Jeremy probably shouldn't venture out alone. What if his ribs started to hurt?

"A walk outside would be really nice right now," she said instead.

A few minutes later, they'd both tugged on coats and stepped outside. Huge puddles of water still filled any and all low-lying areas. The gray sky promised more rain.

In other words, it was going to be a long week.

Jeremy paused as soon as they stepped out the door and nodded toward her backyard. "Is that a graveyard?"

She smiled. She got that reaction from her guests

here at the inn a lot. "It is. When the winds here shift, we never know what we're going to discover. About fifteen years ago, a storm whipped up the sand here on the island and uncovered those tombstones."

"Fascinating."

"It is, really. The dates go back to the early eighteen hundreds. I'm not the only one with tombstones on my property. It's happened to several people throughout the years."

"I'll have to figure out a way to use that in one of my screenplays . . . I've never seen anything like it."

"You'll have to do that."

"You said there are others on the island?"

She nodded. "There sure are. Cemeteries are scattered all over this sandy stretch of land."

He pointed to something else. "And what's that on top of those tombstones?"

"The eelgrass?" Emmy questioned. "I call that East Coast Tumbleweed. It gets blown over from the Currituck Sound during storms. I actually did a research paper on it when I was in high school. It used to be used as insulation in houses, to pack shellfish, and even as a cushion when burying people."

"You're a wealth of information."

She shrugged. "I find things like that fascinating."

They walked for several minutes in silence. A winter wind whipped around them, chilling Emmy's nose. But she found the briskness invigorating.

"Listen," Jeremy started as they strolled beside each other. "I know I need to find another place to stay—"

"Don't be silly. You're fine staying at the inn."

He glanced at her. "I feel like I'm imposing."

"Your ribs are fractured, your leg has a cut, you're recovering from a concussion . . . and it's my fault. Staying at the inn is the least I can do."

He stole another look at her. "Are you sure? I can pay you—"

She waved him off. "Don't be silly. I'm not worried about that. I'm just glad that you're okay. How long were you planning on staying in town?"

"A couple of weeks."

"Then consider the inn your home while you're here."

"That's very generous of you."

She shrugged. "I'm just sorry you've gone through all this."

"So, tell me about yourself, Emmy," Jeremy said

as they continued to walk beside each other. "You must really like island life here."

"I can't imagine living anywhere else." She shoved her hands into her coat pockets as she skirted the edge of a puddle.

"It does seem rather peaceful here." Jeremy glanced around, almost as if seeing this place for the first time.

"It usually is . . . except when it's flooding, of course," Emmy said.

That got a smile out of him.

"How about you?" Emmy asked. "Is this your first time here?"

"It is. I've heard about this place. It's going to be perfect for my new screenplay. Maybe this will be the one that actually sells."

"Is screenwriting all you do or do you have another job as well?"

"You mean a job that pays the bills?" He smiled. "I do some computer programming. But I've taken a leave of absence so I can finish this project. Sure, money is tight, but I manage to get by. I just can't live an extravagant lifestyle. Maybe a place like this would be good for me."

"I think a place like this is good for a lot of

people. I think the fresh ocean air is good for the soul."

They climbed to the top of a dune and peered out at the ocean on the other side.

"Would you look at that?" Jeremy pointed to something in the distance.

Two stallions charged at each other on the edge of the waves.

"What are they doing?" Jeremy asked. "Shouldn't you stop them?"

"As soon as we touch a wild horse, the animal has to go into captivity. So we try not to do that unless it's absolutely necessary, usually in the case of a horse being injured. I know it looks bad when two horses go at each other, but this is just nature's way."

"What are they fighting over?"

"Those are two stallions. One is Clover and the other is Pudding. They're most likely fighting over a mare for their harem or territories."

"Harem?"

Emmy smiled. "I know it sounds funny, but that's what they're called. Every stallion has five or six lady friends that are theirs and theirs alone, for lack of a better way to describe it."

"And they actually fight to see who will get to be whose, huh?"

She stared at the two horses as they went at each other again. "This is just the nature of the horses."

"I kind of like it," Jeremy said. "Maybe we should start doing that as humans. Fighting for what we believe in like that, you know?"

She chuckled. "In some ways, yes. That makes perfect sense. But I'm not a huge fan of violence."

"Right. I don't mean violence. It's like you said, just fighting for the things that are important to you. Not giving up too easily. I can stand by those things."

The two of them exchanged a smile.

But as Emmy looked away, tension threaded up her spine.

She recognized the feeling—the feeling of being watched.

Her hand went to her neck as she glanced around, looking for the source of her stress.

No one was within eyesight. But there were several patches of trees and bushes nearby. Could there be someone hiding in one of those patches?

She didn't know.

She only knew she needed to head back to the inn.

Now.

CHAPTER ELEVEN

"WHO'S THE GUY WITH EMMY?" Grant asked.

"Jeremy Riesling." Colby hated even saying his name.

Colby and Grant stood inside the doorway of the Community Safety building. This vantage point was perfect to watch Jeremy and Emmy walking back to the inn. Every time Emmy laughed at something Jeremy said, a knot grew in Colby's stomach.

He couldn't let himself feel jealous. It was ridiculous.

Just because the man was staying at Emmy's didn't mean that anything would happen between them. Emmy had always been very adamant about how much she loved being single. Who said this one guy was going to change her mind? He wasn't that special.

Colby wasn't being fair, and he knew that. He needed to do better.

"Did the two of them know each other before this?" Grant asked.

Colby's irritation wanted to rise to the surface again, but he held it back. "No, they didn't."

"Watching them talk right now, they almost look like old friends, don't they?"

"I wouldn't say that," Colby scoffed.

Grant studied him for a minute. "Well, I'll be a rooting, tooting fool . . . you, Colby Morris, are jealous."

"Why would I be jealous?"

"Oh, I don't know." Grant shrugged. "Maybe you should tell Emmy how you feel about her."

Colby shook his head. "Why does everyone think that?"

"Because to say otherwise would be hogwash."

Colby frowned. "Even if that was true, if I were to tell her something like that, it would ruin our friendship."

"Or it could turn it into something great."

His back muscles tightened. "I can't take that

risk. Emmy has been there for me when nobody else has been. I can't take the chance of losing her."

Grant didn't say anything for a moment until finally, "Did the talk you had with your father not go well?"

"No talk with my father ever goes well. At least he wasn't drunk this time."

"Why did he stop by? Just for a friendly visit?"

"Kind of," Colby said. "He didn't ask for money, for once. Maybe he's learned I won't give it to him. I'll buy him groceries but that's it. He'll just buy more alcohol if I give him cash."

"I'm sorry to hear that."

"Strange thing is, this time he said he was changing, giving up drinking, and he was going to prove to me that he could be a better man."

"Sounds like a good starting point."

"If only I hadn't heard it before . . ." Colby frowned.

"It all seems like malarkey to you?"

"Yes, it does."

"Maybe one day he won't disappoint you."

Just then, Levi pulled up to the station. He parked his Jeep beside the building before striding toward them.

"You'll never guess where I just came from."

Colby braced himself. How much weirder could things get?

On second thought, he should never ask himself that question.

"While I was out on patrol, someone flagged me down to tell me that one of the graves in front of Mr. Henderson's house has been dug up."

"Well, I'll be a monkey's uncle. What do you mean?" Grant asked. "Is anything missing?"

"As far as we can tell, no. The original inhabitant is still in the coffin. But somebody was obviously looking for something."

Colby drew in a long, deep breath.

Yet another mystery on their island.

Didn't they already have enough going on without adding this to their growing list?

Obviously, someone didn't think so.

***

"YOU'RE A FUNNY MAN, JEREMY RIESLING." Emmy leaned against the kitchen counter, waiting for her casserole to finish cooking. Jeremy sat at the kitchen table, entertaining her with stories about people he'd met while doing research.

He was really quite entertaining.

She stopped mid-laugh when she heard her front door open.

Her heart pounded in her ears when she saw Colby standing there. "Colby . . . glad you could join us."

Colby's gaze flickered to Jeremy, and he offered a stiff nod as he stomped closer to them. "You know me—I never miss dinner."

"I was just getting ready to pull some shepherd's pie from the oven. How's that sound?"

"It sounds great."

"It's one of Jeremy's favorites," Emmy added.

Was it her imagination or did Colby's gaze darken? Emmy really hoped that he still wasn't in his overprotective mood. Jeremy posed absolutely no threat to her. He was just as much a victim as she was.

"How are you feeling today?" Colby asked Jeremy as he rigidly stood against the wall in the kitchen.

"Doing good. Still a little stiff, but, overall, I should be fine."

"That's good news. I'm sure we can help you find a new rental house for while you're in town."

Emmy threw him a startled look. Was he still trying to get this man out of the inn?

"I thought it might be easier, actually, if I stayed

here for a while." Jeremy shrugged. "Besides, it's nice to have someone to talk to. Emmy is quite the muse for me. I had a few good hours of writing today that I wouldn't have had if it wasn't for her."

"Is that right?" Colby's neck looked taut.

Emmy could tell that he didn't like that news.

She needed to change the subject before things became even more awkward.

Using her oven mitts, she grabbed the casserole dish from the oven and placed it on the table. "Let's eat."

With three of them at the table, they lifted a prayer before dinner was served.

But before anyone took a bite, Emmy glanced at her window—just in time to see a shadow there.

CHAPTER TWELVE

"WHAT IS IT?" Colby's entire body tensed.

Emmy pointed at her kitchen window. "Somebody was standing there. Just now."

"What?" Colby rushed to his feet so quickly that his chair fell behind him.

Wasting no time, he strode toward the door. He looked out it just in time to see someone fleeing into the woods.

The driving rain had started again, but that wasn't going to stop Colby.

He took off after the man.

Colby was quick and nimble, but this guy had a head start. Maybe too much of a head start.

The rain and the darkness didn't help. He had to be careful also—if this was the same guy he'd encountered earlier, he wouldn't hesitate to hit Colby over the head with something.

As the brush grew thicker, Colby slowed.

Where had the man gone?

He paused and glanced around.

It was no use.

He'd lost the man's trail.

He frowned.

Why had someone been watching Emmy? What did he want from her?

Colby didn't know . . . and he didn't like this.

EMMY WAS on edge as she waited for Colby to get back.

Was he okay out there?

Maybe she should have gone with him.

But it was too late for that now.

"You're certain you saw someone in the window?" Jeremy asked, rubbing a hand against his dark beard.

"He was looking in the window at us."

"Did you get a glimpse of him?"

Emmy shook her head. "No, his face was shadowed. Maybe he was even wearing a mask. It all happened so quickly, I couldn't tell . . ."

Jeremy let out a breath and shook his head. "Why would someone do that?"

"That's a great question. I really don't know."

"Did I hear you say there was a dead man found here on the island? Murdered?" His skin looked a little paler.

"That's right. The police haven't figured out who the man is or who might have killed him. They're still searching for evidence."

Just then, the door opened and Colby strode back inside. He was soaking wet and dirty—but alive.

Emmy stepped closer, her throat burning with concern. "Colby?"

He shook his head. "He got away. I'm sorry. He had too much of a head start."

"I'm just glad you're okay." She took his arm. "Why don't you go in my room and get cleaned up. You have some extra clothes in the trunk in there."

"I think I will. Thank you."

He disappeared into the room.

"He keeps extra clothes here?" Jeremy asked.

Emmy shrugged, realizing how that might sound. "He's here a lot. Finally, I just told him to keep a few extras at my place, for occasions. . . like this."

"Do things like this happen often?"

Emmy shook her head. "No, not really. But I believe in being prepared."

But there was nothing that could prepare her for the fear she felt when she considered all that had happened over the past couple of days.

CHAPTER THIRTEEN

A FEW MINUTES LATER, Colby was back out, wearing some clean jeans and a sweatshirt. But the worried look still laced his gaze.

This whole situation had him shaken up, didn't it?

Emmy couldn't blame him. She was scared too.

Something bad was going on in Cape Corral.

They had a dead man to prove it.

"So, are there any updates that you're allowed to share?" Emmy asked Colby once they were at the kitchen table again.

The conversation seemed too normal. But what else could they talk about?

"I've been curious also," Jeremy said before taking a bite of his shepherd's pie. "It sounded like yesterday was pretty exciting around here. And let me say, this casserole is delicious."

"Thank you," Emmy said.

"It's been interesting, to say the least." Colby poked his fork into his food but didn't try it otherwise. "Lots of things happening."

He glanced at Jeremy, and Emmy knew there was something Colby couldn't share in front of her guest.

But she wondered exactly what was going on.

Jeremy seemed to sense their unspoken conversation. He glanced at his watch and stood. "You know what? I need to run up to my room and take my pain medication. I'll be right back."

As soon as Jeremy disappeared, Colby turned toward her.

Emmy prayed he didn't have terribly bad news .. . because she couldn't handle any more of that.

"My dad stopped by the station today," Colby shared.

"Is that right?" Emmy knew all about the rocky relationship the two of them shared. It had been that way ever since Emmy could remember.

Colby's mom had left them when Colby was only a toddler. After that, Colby's father began drinking even more. The man was as mean as a snake after a few drinks. Eventually, he turned into a funny drunk.

By then, the damage was usually done.

Colby had practically grown up at Emmy's place instead. He came over almost every night for dinner or just to hang out with the family. Emmy's father—who'd acted as the chief law enforcement officer on the island until Levi took over—had let Colby hang out at the station and had showed him what it meant to be a true saltwater cowboy. Levi thought of him as a little brother.

Not many people knew that Colby was the only person who'd helped Emmy in her grief when her mom had passed away from a heart attack when Emmy was only nine.

He'd understood her loss, and he'd let her cry on his shoulder.

That was something she would never forget. Their grief had bonded them.

"This is what the rest of my life is going to look like." Colby ran a hand over his face, unable to hide the tension across his jaw. "My father getting drunk, and me trying to clean up his messes."

She squeezed his hand. "I'm sorry, Colby. I wish things were different. I really do."

"It is what it is. Isn't that how the saying goes?

Now, why talk about my father when we can talk about just how delicious your food is?"

THE REST OF DINNER, they kept the chitchat generic. Jeremy asked some questions about the island, which seemed like a safe enough subject. Rain had started outside and a wind had kicked up, rattling the walls of the inn.

After they cleaned up, Colby touched Emmy's arm. "You feel like going outside to sit on the porch and talk for a minute?"

Emmy frowned. "That sounds really nice. But I told Jeremy that we could play Scrabble. Do you want to play with us?"

Colby's face remained tense. "No, why don't you go play? I'll be fine."

"Colby . . . what's going on with you?"

"What do you mean? Nothing's going on with me."

"That's not the vibe I'm getting from you."

He shrugged. "Maybe we're all just tired."

She stepped closer. "Colby Morris, I know you better than you know yourself. Something is definitely wrong."

"I think I just need to get some sleep."

"Have you slept yet?"

He shook his head. "Only if you count the hour I dozed off at the station."

"You need to get some sleep." That was just the kind of guy Colby was. He was a hard worker who poured himself into whatever project he was working on.

He was also the kind of guy who loved getting people together for bonfires. Who was fun but loved deep relationships. Who led a Bible study at his home every week. He even took a local scouting group on a camping trip every year.

But right now, he needed to think about himself.

He'd had a long, long night, Emmy mused.

Was he still worried about that note found on the dead man? Was he still worried that Emmy could be in danger?

There was nothing to prove that was the case.

Colby nodded again before his gaze slipped to Jeremy in the background. "I'll let you two get started on your game. If you need anything, call me. If you see anything, call me. If you hear anything, call me."

"Message has been received." Emmy tried to break the tension by offering a salute.

Colby stepped closer. "I mean it. I'm worried about you. I don't know what's going on, and I don't like it."

Her smile faded. "Believe me, I'll call you at the first sign anything is wrong. I promise."

He stared at her another moment, almost as if he wanted to say more.

Instead, he took a step back. "Goodnight, Emmy."

"Goodnight, Colby."

As Colby left, Emmy couldn't help but feel empty inside.

Why was her best friend acting distant? Was it his dad again?

Nothing got Colby upset faster than his father.

Emmy wanted to reach out to him. To try to comfort him. To wrap her arms around him in a hug.

But now wasn't a good time.

Later, she promised herself.

They would have a nice, long talk . . . later. And she would get this all figured out.

But, until then, she knew she would feel unsettled.

CHAPTER FOURTEEN

JUST AS COLBY drifted off to sleep, his phone rang.

"We've got another fire," Dillon said. "We need you at the station."

Moving quickly, Colby grabbed his gear from his truck, slipped it on, and rushed to the station. He arrived in less than five minutes. As soon as he got there, he climbed into the fire truck where four volunteer firefighters waited.

"Where is it this time?" Colby asked Dillon as they started down the road.

"It's at another house on the North Banks." Dillon's steely face looked even harder as he said the words.

Colby's heart went still. "Another one of the Fergusons' places? Again?"

"That's what it appears."

Colby knew what that meant. Someone was targeting the family.

But who? And why?

In the distance, Colby saw flames licking the roof of a house.

This wasn't a good sign.

He braced himself for a long night and prayed that no one was hurt.

Four hours later, the fire was out. But the place was still too hot for them to go inside and investigate. That would have to wait until the morning.

As Colby looked at the carnage of what had happened, a sick feeling formed in his gut.

A dead man with Emmy's address in his pocket. A grave that had been disturbed. And a building that had been scorched.

He wasn't naive enough to think that the three weren't connected.

But how?

Movement in the distance caught his eye.

Thomas Ferguson, the patriarch of the Ferguson clan, stormed across the sand, his figure illuminated by the lights that had been set up in the area.

"I don't think you're taking these fires seriously enough!" the man lashed out at Levi and Dillon.

"I assure you, we're taking this very seriously," Levi said.

"You and your men are probably in on this, for that matter!"

Colby's back muscles tensed. He knew Levi and Dillon could handle themselves, but Colby didn't like the way this was going down.

"We may not agree with your agenda for the island, but we'd never try to hurt you or your family," Dillon said.

"You can't prove that by me!" Ferguson fisted his hands as if he might strike.

Colby braced himself to step in.

Before things escalated, a truck pulled up beside them and someone jumped out. Abigail Ferguson, Thomas' youngest daughter, rushed toward her father, concern etched into the lines across her forehead.

"Daddy, don't!" Abigail placed a hand on his arm, pleading with him. "You need to cool down. You're not thinking clearly."

"I know exactly what I'm thinking!" Ferguson glared at Levi and Dillon. "This town is determined to push us out. But I'm not going to let that happen!"

Before anyone could say anything else, Mr. Ferguson stormed away. Abigail cast an apologetic glance at everyone before following after her dad.

Colby felt the tension mounting here on the island. He wondered when it would reach its peak and explode.

When that happened, things were going to turn even uglier than they were now.

They had to find the person behind these arsons and stop him before Cape Corral imploded.

CHAPTER FIFTEEN

THE NEXT MORNING, Emmy awoke early to bake some muffins. She left a couple for Jeremy, and then she put the rest in the basket and walked across the sand to the Community Safety building. There were advantages to living so close.

She often liked to bring food to the guys, partly because Levi was her brother and Colby was her best friend. It just made sense to try to take care of them.

She'd heard the commotion at the station last night. Heard the sirens. She knew that something else had happened.

Part of her couldn't wait to find out what. Not because she wanted things to happen on the island. But, if they did, Emmy wanted to know about them.

Her relatives went back generations on Cape Corral. In some ways, she felt like this land was her own. Maybe that was one reason why it was so hard for her to see all the changes that had started to come to the place lately.

Ever since the Fergusons had moved to town, all she heard about was how people wanted to develop the island more. Couldn't they see what a terrible idea it was? The wild horses needed their space. They needed room to breathe.

Emmy needed room to breathe.

The rain had started again—but hopefully this would be the last day. She dodged the puddles outside as she raced across the sand toward the front door.

Finally, she stepped inside and pulled off the hood of her sweatshirt.

She glanced around and called, "Hello!"

A moment later, Colby poked his head out from the break room down the hallway.

He looked even worse today than he had yesterday. Circles darkened the skin beneath his eyes. His hair looked even more tousled than usual. His shirt was wrinkled.

Emmy met him halfway across the space. She placed her basket on a table before throwing her arms around his neck, pulling him close for a hug. "You look terrible."

"Only you can get away with saying that."

She stepped back and nodded at the basket. "I brought some cranberry muffins."

"They always make everything better." He smiled before glancing behind her. "Where is your new friend?"

"You mean my *guest*?"

"He looks like more than a guest to me," Colby said.

Her hands went to her hips. "Now, Colby. You're not thinking that I'm trying to stir up some romance with one of my guests, are you?"

He shrugged. "The thought did cross my mind."

"I'm simply trying to make up for my mistakes. I hit the poor man. I can't send him out into the wild. You wouldn't do that to one of our horses here, now would you?"

He rubbed his chin. "I suppose I wouldn't."

"That's what I thought." Emmy looped her arm through his, and they started walking toward his office. "How about we have a muffin and catch up for a few minutes?"

"That sounds like a great idea."

Emmy could use a moment of normal to combat

this crazy week.

But, no matter how she looked at it, her uneasiness wouldn't subside.

That nor'easter wasn't the only thing on the horizon.

So was danger. She could feel it in her bones.

The question was: what would the aftermath be?

COLBY'S DAY was brightened just by the fact that Emmy had stopped by to spend some time with him. The two of them were still talking in his office when Levi stepped inside.

Emmy stood and gave her brother a quick hug. "How's it going?"

Levi's gaze darkened. "Could be better."

"Could be better? But you and Dani are married now. What could be better than that?"

He let out a chuckle, his gaze lightening at the sound of his wife's name. "That's true. That aspect of my life is going very well, I must say. But in matters of things here on the island, it could be better."

Emmy frowned. "Any updates on the dead man?"

"None. We still haven't identified him, where he was staying, or how he got to the island. We've yet to find the murder weapon, any witnesses, or any motives for why someone may have killed him. And we still have no idea why your address was in his pocket."

Colby frowned. "That's too bad."

"It really is."

"What was he even doing out there at Smith's Hope?" Emmy asked.

"Another good question," Levi said. "At first, I thought he was illegally hunting. But he didn't have any hunting equipment on him."

Emmy narrowed her eyes. "You said he called 911, right?"

"He did—said he hurt his leg," Colby said. "When we got there, his phone was gone. I'm surprised we even found your address on him— probably only because it was in a pocket on the front of his shirt."

"So weird . . ." Emmy shook her head.

"What about the grave that was dug up?" Colby hadn't had a chance to catch up with Levi yet. All of them had been so busy with everything going on.

"It appears that nothing is missing. No one has any idea why somebody would have dug it up. Some people think that it was just some teenagers playing pranks."

"But what do you think?" Emmy asked.

Levi pressed his lips together. "I think there's more going on here than meets the eye. And I'm going to get to the bottom of it."

"You just let me know what I can do," Colby said.

Levi nodded. "I'll do that. For now just keep my sister entertained and out of trouble."

"It's a full-time job." Colby winked at Emmy.

"I don't know who you boys think you are, but I'm the one who's keeping you two out of trouble." She snapped her fingers and used her most southern voice to say, "And ain't nobody in town going to deny that."

They both chuckled because they knew her words were true.

Colby's theory was only confirmed yet again.

Everything was always better when Emmy was around.

Yet he could feel that part of his world beginning to shift, and he felt powerless to stop it.

WHEN EMMY LEFT THE STATION, she paused as she walked back to her house and stared at her

Dodge that was parked beside her house, left there earlier by Colby.

The truck that had hit Jeremy.

The one that had also been rifled through afterward.

Her heart pounded a little harder.

On a whim, Emmy climbed behind the steering wheel and slammed the door. She sat in silence for a moment.

The interior looked normal.

If she had to guess, Colby had straightened everything up for her. His goal in life seemed to be taking care of her like that.

But it still didn't make sense why someone had gone through her things in the first place. Emmy had nothing of value. And, if she had, then she definitely wouldn't keep it in her truck.

She frowned and reached for the glove compartment. Opening it, she looked through the papers there. It was mostly her registration and a truck manual. An old tube of lip balm was also tucked in there, as well as some sea glass Colby had given her.

Emmy smiled when she remembered the day Colby had found it.

They'd been strolling along the beach, talking about life and the future and their dreams. Colby had moved some shells with his foot. When he did, he found a beautiful piece of turquoise sea glass—one of the rarest and most sought-after colors.

He hadn't hesitated to give it to Emmy so they could always remember their talk.

Emmy kept it in the truck because she liked to find it there, to be reminded of her friendship with Colby.

Right now, she rubbed the glass in her hands before pressing it to her heart.

Almost every memory she had here on the island involved Colby. Their lives were intertwined in so many ways.

Colby was almost like having a boyfriend without all the complications of a relationship. It was the best of both worlds. In fact, having Colby by her side made it easier to be single. Who needed to date when Colby was always there for her?

Emmy hated seeing how burdened he looked today.

This would pass, she reminded herself.

The flooding would cease, they'd solve the island's mysteries, and life would return to normal.

Why did she doubt her own reassurances?

Maybe she would be a fool not to.

CHAPTER SIXTEEN

COLBY WAS WORKING out in the small gym at the station when his phone rang.

He hadn't seen the name on the screen for a long time.

He pushed himself upright on the weight bench and put the phone to his ear. "Luke. How's it going?"

"Good to talk to you, bro. How's it going down there in Cape Corral?"

"It's wet. The whole island feels like it's sinking."

Luke chuckled. "I remember what that was like. Those nor'easters can mess you up."

"Yes, they can."

Luke had grown up here but had moved after he graduated from high school. He'd joined the National Guard and eventually settled in the

Hampton Roads area of Virginia. The two still talked once or twice a year.

"Listen, I thought I'd let you know that I'm starting my own business," Luke continued.

"That's great, man. Congrats." Colby grabbed a towel and wiped his forehead, wondering where his friend was going with this.

"The thing is I could really use some reliable help. I got my general contractor's license, and I'm starting to work on some home renovations in the area."

"Sounds exciting. I can't say I know anyone looking for work, though."

Luke paused for just a moment. "I was hoping you might be interested."

Colby blanched. "Me? I'm not a contractor."

"No, but you've always been good with your hands and a hard worker. You were the first person I thought about. I wondered if you had any desire to get away from that little island."

Leave Cape Corral? Colby had never really thought about it—never considered it, for that matter. "I don't know . . ."

"Listen, think about it," Luke continued. "I know this is out of the blue. But it could be a really good job opportunity. I'd love to have you on board."

"Good to know."

As the call ended, Colby continued to think about the conversation.

Leave Cape Corral?

That would mean leaving Emmy.

Colby wasn't sure he could ever do that.

But how long could he hide his feelings from his best friend?

THAT EVENING, Emmy sat up straight in bed. What was that?

A noise had awoken her.

She remembered the guest staying with her. Jeremy.

The man had probably just gotten up to go to the bathroom. There was nothing to worry about.

With all the drama happening on the island right now, Emmy's senses were on higher alert than usual.

She couldn't stop thinking about everything she'd learned about: her truck being rifled through, the dead body Colby and Dillon had discovered, the note with her address on it, the fires on the Ferguson properties.

Things felt like a mess. Everywhere.

But in other ways, Emmy couldn't complain. She was doing a job she treasured in a place that she adored with people she loved.

What was there to grumble about?

Nothing.

Another creak sounded nearby.

That was definitely movement.

But Emmy didn't think it was coming from above her. Maybe it wasn't inside after all. Could the sound have come from her porch?

She didn't know. But she wouldn't get any sleep until she found out.

She threw on her sweatshirt and some sneakers. At the last moment, she grabbed the gun from her nightstand. She was a country girl, and she'd been raised to know how to take care of herself.

Usually, at least.

With one last glance at her alarm clock—which read three a.m.—she quietly stepped from her room and into the dark hallway.

She must have been sleeping hard because it didn't feel like three a.m. She felt like she'd just fallen asleep.

She and Jeremy had played another game this evening—Scrabble. Emmy had expected more from him since he was a screenwriter, but she'd beat him both times. Despite that, the man's recovery seemed to be coming along well.

Emmy had discovered he was great company—a good conversationalist who knew how to make her laugh. They'd played Christmas music and had eaten homemade fudge.

The man was certainly intriguing and entertaining. In fact, he nearly made her forget about the problems here on the island.

Despite the fun they'd had, Jeremy wasn't Colby. There was something about the camaraderie between Emmy and Colby that could never be replicated—nor did Emmy ever want it to be.

Quietly, she crept up the stairs.

When she reached the top, she saw the door to Jeremy's room was wide open.

As trepidation stretched across her chest, Emmy tiptoed closer and peered inside.

His bed was empty, the white coverlet thrown back as if he'd suddenly gotten up.

Emmy turned to look at the bathroom behind her.

That door was also open.

If Jeremy wasn't in his room or in the bathroom, where was he?

The question made uneasiness slosh inside her.

As she walked back downstairs, she checked each door as she passed.

If Jeremy wasn't in the house, then that meant he'd left.

But the front door was locked. She checked.

Moving slowly, quietly, Emmy continued to the back door.

She twisted it and let out a breath.

It was unlocked.

She was certain she'd locked it before going to bed. Even though the island was generally safe, locking her door was something her dad had taught her was important.

Emmy pulled out her phone and turned on the flashlight.

She swept the beam across her backyard, searching for any clues of where Jeremy may have gone. Maybe he was simply sitting on her back deck.

But she didn't see anybody out there.

Everything seemed strangely quiet.

Something out of place in the distance caught her eye.

What was that? It was hard to see from where she stood, but something glimmered in the occasional lightning. Whatever it was, the object was located between the tombstones lining the back of her yard.

Emmy knew she probably shouldn't check, that she should call Levi or Colby.

But both of them had looked so sleepy. They needed their rest.

Whatever that object was, it was probably nothing.

But if it was nothing, why couldn't Emmy stop staring?

She had to know what it was.

Besides, what if Jeremy was in trouble? What if he had taken a late-night walk and had fallen?

With that in her mind, she stepped out the door. As soon as it creaked shut behind her, more tension tugged at her muscles.

She hoped that she wouldn't regret this.

"Jeremy?" she called.

But only the wind and rain answered back.

Big fat drops of water fell from the sky. Some of today's earlier precipitation still remained in low-lying areas. But Emmy's backyard, for the most part, was absent of any flooding overwash or puddles.

She crept forward, pulling her sweatshirt closer.

Even though she knew this was a bad idea, she couldn't stop.

This was her property, and nobody was going to mess with her.

"Jeremy?" she called again.

Still no answer.

She skulked deeper into her backyard. As she did, she squinted.

Was that a pile of . . . sand and dirt?

She shuffled toward it, wondering if she was seeing things.

But it almost appeared that someone had been digging a hole in her backyard.

What sense would that make?

Just as she started to reach for her gun, she heard a sound behind her.

The next instant, someone shoved her.

The gun flew from her hands as Emmy began falling.

Into a dirt pit.

No, not a dirt pit.

Into an unearthed grave.

CHAPTER SEVENTEEN

EMMY SUCKED in a breath as she felt the mud and grit at her fingertips. When she felt the wood beneath her. When she felt the slick walls surrounding her.

She glanced up at the dark sky overhead.

She halfway expected a face to appear above her, taunting her, finishing what he'd started.

But no one came.

Someone had clearly been in her backyard.

The man had shoved her.

But who? And why?

If only she had her gun to protect herself with.

Her heart pounded in her ears at the thought.

Instead, she felt helpless.

Emmy scrambled to her feet as she realized that she was sitting on something.

Something wooden.

And old.

And rotting.

She gasped as realization hit her.

She was on top of a coffin.

Her heart beat faster.

What was going on here?

Emmy had to get out of here.

Now.

She tried to claw her way up the walls. But it was too muddy. Her feet kept slipping.

There had to be something else she could do.

Her phone, she realized.

She needed to find her phone.

She'd been using the flashlight when someone shoved her.

But she must have dropped it, along with her gun, when she fell.

Where was it now?

Drawing in a deep breath and every ounce of courage, Emmy leaned down and began feeling around the sandy dirt. As the rough wood of the old coffin scratched her fingertips, her muscles tightened.

She wasn't superstitious or even easily spooked.

But this had her unnerved.

"Please, let me find it," she whispered. "Please, let me find it."

She prayed the fervent prayers, hoping that God would be on her side.

But she didn't find her phone.

That didn't mean that God wasn't on her side. But it did mean she was going to have to think of something different here.

As more fat drops of rain hit her face, she realized the storm was coming closer.

She could *not* be in this grave when the sky opened.

There was no way.

Instead, Emmy cupped her hands around her mouth and yelled, "Help! Help me!"

COLBY RETURNED to the station after being called to rescue someone who'd been stuck in flood waters down by the clinic. At least he'd gotten a few hours of sleep before the call came in.

He was walking toward his truck when he heard something.

He froze.

Was that someone yelling "help me"?

Tension threaded between his muscles.

In two seconds flat, he sprinted toward Emmy's place. That was her. He knew it was.

He paused at the edge of her backyard, "Emmy?"

"Over here!"

As he ran toward her voice, he nearly collided with somebody.

Jeremy.

"I heard someone yelling . . ." the man muttered.

Colby bristled and didn't resist scowling. But he didn't have time to deal with this man right now.

"Stay there!" he grumbled instead.

The best thing this man could do was keep out of his way.

Colby glanced through the darkness, trying to find his friend. "Emmy?"

"I'm down here!"

He stepped between some tombstones and peered down.

Emmy stood inside a dug-up grave.

Colby's heart pounded in his chest at the realization. "Emmy? What happened?"

"Someone pushed me in." Emmy's eyes looked wide with fear. "Get me out of here. Please."

Pushed her in? A surge of anger went up his spine.

He'd deal with that later.

Right now, Colby lowered himself onto his chest and reached into the sandy pit. Emmy grabbed his arm, and he helped her scale the slippery side of the hole. A moment later, she landed beside him on the wet ground.

"Thank you." She drew in a ragged breath as she stared up at him, mud covering half of her face. "I'm so glad you heard me yelling."

Colby's heart continued to race. "I'm glad I heard you too . . . or you may have had a different outcome."

As he said the words, the sky broke open even more. More buckets of rain flooded down.

Colby rose to his feet and extended his hand to Emmy. "Let's get inside. Then we need to talk."

CHAPTER EIGHTEEN

EMMY QUICKLY TOOK a shower and changed, trying to get the mud off her. She wished it was that easy to wash her fear away.

But tonight's event would remain with her for a long time.

As she cleaned herself up, Emmy knew that Colby was calling Levi to tell him what had happened. They would be looking for the person who did this to her.

Her heart still pounded with fear. It had been a long time since she had felt that frightened—that was if she didn't include the night she'd hit Jeremy while driving. But that had been a different kind of fear.

She was still drying her hair on an old towel

when she stepped out of her downstairs bedroom. Jeremy sat at the kitchen table, looking like he was preparing himself for an interrogation.

Meanwhile, Colby slipped his phone back into his pocket and turned to her as he lingered in the kitchen. He'd changed into a dry sweatshirt, one he kept in an old armoire here at the inn.

"Are you okay?" His voice sounded soft and prodding.

"I'm fine." She forced a smile. "Just feeling a little bit off my game right now."

"As anyone in your shoes would be," Colby said.

Emmy's gaze shot to Jeremy. He fidgeted as if nervous.

"You mind telling me what happened tonight?" Colby asked.

"I thought I heard something," Emmy started. "I wanted to make sure that everything was okay so I got up to check things out. That's when I noticed that Jeremy was gone, and I worried that something had happened."

Colby's gaze went to Jeremy, and he didn't bother to hide his irritation. "Do you care to explain that?"

Jeremy cringed, still looking uncomfortable. "It's not what you think."

"You mean, you're not the one who dug that hole?" Colby pushed.

"What? Me?" Jeremy's eyebrows shot up. "No. Why would I do that?"

"Why *would* you do that?" Colby asked.

Emmy knew she should step in as she felt the tension rising between the two men.

But her questions echoed Colby's.

What exactly was Jeremy doing outside at three a.m.?

―――

COLBY WATCHED Jeremy's expression carefully. He sensed the man was hiding something—and Colby didn't like it.

"Look, I know how this looks." Jeremy raised his hands up to his chest level, just enough to proclaim innocence. "But I had nothing to do with that hole. Look at me. I'm clean. If I'd dug that hole, there would be dirt all over me."

The man had a point. He was wet, but there wasn't any mud on him.

Colby still wasn't ready to let Jeremy off the hook, though. "Where exactly did you go at this time of night?"

"I'm an insomniac." Jeremy shrugged. "I do some of my best work at night. Sometimes, if I don't feel the words flowing, it helps me if I take a walk."

"So you just left to take a stroll at three a.m.?" Emmy's eyebrows scrunched together as if she didn't understand either.

"I didn't want to wake you up." Jeremy shrugged again, exhaustion etched into his features. "So I tried to be quiet. I guess I failed. I'm really sorry about that. I never imagined all of this . . ."

"And you just happened to be returning from your walk when Emmy fell in a grave that had been recently dug up?"

"That's right. I wanted to walk a little farther, but I felt rain and turned around. I was coming in from the opposite direction of the station when I heard someone yelling."

"It's an interesting story," Colby muttered, still not ready to believe him.

Emmy rose, putting herself between the two men as she frowned. "Look, I think tensions are running high here tonight for several reasons. What we really need to concentrate on right now is finding the real person who dug up the grave and pushed me in. Then we need to figure out why."

Colby crossed his arms, his jaw still hard. "I agree that that's a good idea."

"If you two don't need me anymore, I think I will go back up to my room and get out of your hair," Jeremy said. "It seems like I've caused enough trouble tonight."

"Levi might want to talk to you," Colby reminded him. "He's going to need to investigate."

Jeremy frowned as he rose to his feet. "I'm sure I'll be awake, so if he needs to speak with me, then please send him up. I'm sorry that you fell into that hole tonight, Emmy. But I am glad you are okay."

Colby watched the man walk away. As soon as Jeremy was gone from sight, relief filled him—relief because Colby finally had a moment alone with Emmy. But the emotion was short lived as tension quickly took its place.

Because Jeremy was still going to be staying here.

With Emmy.

And with everything going on here on this island, that wasn't something that Colby was comfortable with.

CHAPTER NINETEEN

AS JEREMY DISAPPEARED up the steps, Emmy turned to Colby. "You don't have to be so hard on him."

Colby's expression darkened. "I'm not trying to be hard on him. I just don't want to see you in a bad situation. And it *is* suspicious that Jeremy was out tonight when all of this went down."

Emmy made a gun with her hand and pointed it at Colby. "But he had a point when he said his clothes weren't dirty. There's no way he could have dug that grave up and stayed so clean."

Colby looked like he didn't quite believe her observation. Emmy knew him well enough to know that he was probably trying to figure out a way

Jeremy could have managed to both dig the hole *and* stay clean.

Emmy appreciated her friend's concern for her. But she couldn't help but think that Colby was over-reacting.

Before they could talk about it much longer, someone lightly knocked before stepping in through the back door.

Levi.

He wiped his feet on the mat and stripped off his jacket, which was soaking wet from the downpour outside. He hung it on the coat stand before walking toward Emmy and Colby.

Colby straightened. "You done?"

"For tonight," Levi muttered, lowering himself on the other end of the table. He set Emmy's phone and gun there. "I thought you'd want these back."

"I dropped them when the man pushed me." Emmy frowned.

"You shouldn't have gone outside to begin with. You should have called us before you ventured outside by yourself." Levi narrowed his gaze.

"I know. I just thought . . ." She shook her head. "I don't know what I was thinking."

"Things could have turned out much differently," Levi continued.

"Believe me—I know." Emmy stood, desperate to change the subject. "Now, let me get you some coffee—"

"You sit," Levi said. "I'm fine."

After hesitating a moment, she lowered herself back to the table. "Could you tell anything from looking at the scene?"

Emmy could hardly breathe as she waited for her brother's answer. Maybe if she had some answers, she would stop trembling so badly.

Levi's frown deepened. "Not really. Everything is wet, and the rain isn't working in our favor. Any clues that may have been left outside were washed away. Grant and I tried to set up a tent over the gravesite, but the wind keeps blowing it over."

"This is the second grave that's been dug up in this area." Colby shook his head. "What in the world is going on?"

"That's what I would like to know too." Levi rubbed his jaw. "Neither of you have any idea what's going on?"

"I have no clue." Emmy pulled the sleeves of her sweatshirt over her hands, unable to get warm. "Best I can tell, that grave hasn't been touched in more than one hundred years. Why would someone try to dig it up now?"

"That's the question we're all asking," Levi said. "And what does this have to do with our dead man, if anything?"

"I wish I knew," Colby said.

Levi's gaze flickered to the stairs where Jeremy had just disappeared moments earlier. "What about your guest?"

Emmy shrugged and repeated what Jeremy had told her about being an insomniac. She finished with, "He said you're welcome to go up and talk to him if you'd like."

Levi nodded slowly. "Actually, I *would* like a few words with him. Excuse me."

As soon as her brother disappeared upstairs, Emmy turned to Colby.

She had a feeling that her friend had something on his mind, and she braced herself for whatever he had to say.

COLBY'S JAW tensed as he tried to find the right words. He'd never been one who used much finesse, though, and right now probably wouldn't be any different.

His gaze locked on Emmy's. "I don't think you should let that man stay here anymore."

Emmy narrowed her eyes, not trying to hide the fact that she was trying to read the emotions in his gaze. "Colby, what has gotten into you?"

Why was she making this about him? "What do you mean? Nothing's gotten into me."

Her narrowed eyes remained on him. "You're acting weird. Really weird."

Colby shrugged, but the motion felt too tight. Certainly, Emmy would see through him. That was the last thing he wanted.

"I think you're reading too much into things," he told her.

Emmy studied him another moment, almost as if giving Colby the opportunity to speak up and explain himself.

But Colby didn't. Despite his feelings for Emmy —even if he had none—there were still plenty of warning alarms going off about Emmy's newest guest.

Besides, sharing his feelings would do no good.

Emmy had made it clear she wasn't the type of woman who could be boxed in. She had more in common with the wild horses here on the island than she did the domesticated ones. She liked to do what she wanted to do when she wanted to do it.

Those were just some of the qualities that Colby loved about his best friend.

Despite that, Colby would do anything right now to be able to take Emmy into his arms and show her how he really felt. But it was a risk he couldn't take, he reminded himself. There was too much at stake.

He quickly looked away before Emmy read too much in his gaze.

No doubt Emmy knew something was on his mind. Sometimes, it was almost like she knew him better than he knew himself.

Levi stomped down the stairs at that moment—a welcome relief to the strained conversation.

Emmy turned toward her brother, light filling her eyes. She rushed to her feet, and Colby copied the motion.

"What did he say?" Emmy asked.

Levi paused near the table, his face still tight with tension. "Mr. Riesling said he had nothing to do with it, of course. I'll look into his background, just to be on the safe side. But I have no evidence to show he had anything to do with this."

"I think looking into his background is a great idea," Colby said.

Emmy gave him a look that clearly showed she wanted to roll her eyes but didn't. "I think both of you are overthinking this."

"I think you need to get some sleep—with your door locked." Levi gave her a pointed look before kissing her forehead. "Goodnight, sis."

"Goodnight."

After Levi closed the door behind him, Colby turned toward Emmy. He knew he needed to leave also.

But he didn't want to.

Not after everything that had happened.

When he saw Emmy shiver, he grabbed a blanket from the back of the chair and wrapped it around her shoulders. He didn't let go of the edges, but instead pulled her closer.

"You're shaking," he murmured.

"It's been quite a night."

"Yes, it has."

Emmy leaned into him, and Colby folded her into a hug.

They fit so well together.

Couldn't Emmy see that?

"What would I do without you, Colby?" she said quietly into his chest.

"You'd have more food in your house."

She chuckled and pulled away from their embrace.

Colby instantly missed her warmth.

"No one is going to argue with you there." She jabbed him in the stomach.

"Don't hurt your finger."

"Man of Steel?" She raised her eyebrows.

"You know it."

She laughed again. "I just love you, Colby. I always have."

Her words made something warm grow in his heart. Colby knew she just meant them in a friendly way.

But what would it be like if they'd meant more?

Emmy twisted her lips as she looked up at him. "Listen, why don't you sleep in one of the guest rooms? It's a little late for you to leave, and it's pouring rain."

"I think that sounds like a great idea." That way, Colby could keep an eye on her a little longer.

And keep an eye on Jeremy.

CHAPTER TWENTY

THE NEXT MORNING, Emmy kept herself busy cleaning the inn—anything to keep her mind occupied. Colby left early for the station, grabbing a homemade cranberry muffin on the way out.

At ten a.m., Jeremy came downstairs for some coffee before disappearing back upstairs. He said he had a great idea he wanted to work on for his screenplay.

Emmy welcomed the time to herself. She hadn't gotten much sleep last night. Everything that had happened was still on her mind.

Every time she closed her eyes, she pictured herself being in that grave again.

She shivered at the thought.

Even though she hadn't been close to dying, part

of her had felt like death was close. No one else would probably understand it, and it was hard to explain, for that matter.

But she'd felt the danger crackling in the air, felt like something bad was going to happen.

Her dad had always said she had great intuition. And maybe she did. She usually got a good sense about people.

Just then, someone knocked at her door.

Emmy answered and saw her sister-in-law, Dani, standing there, the gray sky spitting a few last specks of rain behind her.

Dani held up a basket in her hands. "I tried my hand at some cookies, and I wanted to bring you some. It's the Cape Corral way."

Emmy grinned and took the basket from her. She couldn't ask for a better sister-in-law. Dani was kind, smart, and she made Levi happy.

"You're learning quickly," Emmy said. "Come on in."

The two of them went into the kitchen.

"Can I get you some coffee?" Emmy asked.

"I'd love some, if it's not too much trouble."

A few minutes later, the two of them were seated at the kitchen table and ready to catch up.

"I heard what happened last night," Dani started,

her fingers hugging her coffee mug. "How are you?"

Emmy shrugged. "I'm hanging in. It could have been worse."

"Is it true that someone pushed you in an old grave? That's crazy."

No one had to tell Emmy that twice. "I know. But at least pushing was all they did. I'm thankful things didn't go any farther."

"Me too." Dani frowned.

Emmy could really use a change in conversation. This was entirely too heavy for her right now. "In other news . . . you look like marriage is treating you well."

Emmy took a sip of her coffee as she glanced at her sister-in-law. She meant the words. Dani was practically glowing and her grin was contagious.

"I'd have to agree." Dani shrugged. "I have no complaints. But I got lucky when I met Levi. He's a great man."

"I am so glad to hear you're happy. And I guess my brother is pretty okay." Emmy winked.

"When are you going to give marriage a try? And don't you hate it when people ask you that?" Dani made a face. "But I'm not taking it back. I really want to know."

"I'll let you pass, only because I like you." Emmy

chuckled and picked up one of the gingerbread cookies Dani had brought with her. "But you know me. I'm perfectly content to be single."

"Your new guest is pretty handsome." She pointed with her eyebrows toward the stairs where Jeremy had disappeared.

"He *is* handsome, but he's only here for a little while and then he'll be gone."

"I see. If all else fails, there's always Colby." Dani grinned before sipping her coffee.

"Colby? He's my best friend."

"Are you saying you've never even thought about what it might be like to date him?" Dani leaned back and waited for her answer.

Emmy's cheeks heated at the thought. The truth was, there had been a few times over the past couple of days when Colby had done something to her heart.

Maybe it was because she'd seen him in the hospital. Maybe it was because the events of this week had made her realize the fragility of life.

She didn't know.

But she scolded herself for feeling anything. Colby was her best friend. She couldn't think of him in romantic terms.

Dani waited for her response.

Emmy cleared her throat. "Maybe I *have* thought about it a few times. But the idea of dating Colby is kind of weird, so I try not to think about that. The two of us have got something good going, something special."

"But what happens one day when one of you gets into a serious relationship?"

Emmy had thought about that question before, and each time, it caused a certain sadness to press on her. She didn't have a great answer for Dani. "I guess we will have to cross that bridge when we get there."

"I have a feeling Colby would like to cross that bridge before you do. And when I say cross that bridge, I don't mean with somebody else. I mean with you." Dani gave her a pointed look.

Emmy nearly snorted. "I am almost certain that Colby is *not* thinking about anything except what he wants to eat next."

Dani chuckled. "He does like to eat, but he is a single guy. Can you blame him?"

Emmy shrugged, her sister-in-law's words heavy on her mind. "I guess there *is* part of me that likes taking care of him."

"And there's definitely a part of Colby that likes being taken care of. Besides, you should see the way he looks at you. It's like you're the only woman in the world."

"Yeah . . . the only woman in the world who will cook for him." Emmy let out a laugh, brushing off her sister-in-law's words.

"I'll let you believe that." Dani raised her eyebrows.

Emmy sighed and leaned back, trying not to think too hard about what Dani said. Her sister-in-law was wrong. Colby had absolutely no interest in her. He liked to date around, although those relationships never turned serious.

Dani shifted in her seat. "Can I ask you a question?"

"Go for it." Emmy took another sip of her coffee, bracing herself for Dani's query. Whenever someone prefaced what they were about to ask by asking permission, it wasn't good.

"Have you ever been in a serious relationship or have you always been perfectly content to be single?"

The question surprised Emmy, but she tried not to let it show on her face.

That was one subject she didn't like to talk about.

"SO, did you look into that Jeremy guy staying at your sister's place?" Colby asked Levi that morning. His gut still told him that the guy was trouble, even though he hadn't seen any proof of it.

"As a matter of fact, I did look into him." Levi ran a hand over his face as he leaned back at his desk.

Colby stepped farther into Levi's office. "And?"

He could hardly wait to hear what Levi had to say. Colby needed a good reason to convince Emmy to kick this guy to the curb.

"And . . . he appears to be clean." Levi shrugged almost apologetically. "He really is a screenwriter. He's from New Hampshire. He doesn't have a criminal record."

Colby frowned. "So he's decent?"

Levi chuckled as he straightened some papers on his desk. "Why do you sound so disappointed?"

Colby shrugged, his semi-good mood turning sour. "I don't know. There's just something about him . . ."

"The only thing you don't like about him is that my sister seems to like him." Levi gave him a pointed look before standing to put a file away.

"You're saying you like him?" If anyone was on Colby's side, he'd expected it to be Emmy's overprotective older brother.

Levi paused and shook his head. "I didn't say that."

"So you sense it too . . ." Colby *knew* it!

"Any visitors on the island right now are suspect in my mind, especially with everything going on." Levi sat down again.

"But Jeremy is *especially* suspect."

Levi chuckled again before turning serious. "I'm keeping my eye on him."

Colby knew he needed to change the subject. "Any other updates on things going on here on the island?"

Levi sat back in his chair and sighed. "I wish there were. We've been trying to find anyone who may have purchased large amounts of any kind of accelerant. There's been nothing. No one has seen anything. Our dead body still hasn't been ID'd. And nothing appears to have been taken from the graves."

Colby frowned. "Maybe the same full moon that's making these tides so crazy is also making people crazy."

Levi locked gazes with him. "Just maybe you're right. Let's hope when the moon phases to Waning Gibbous that things will return to normal."

CHAPTER TWENTY-ONE

"THERE WAS one guy once when I was in high school." Emmy leaned back in her seat, her mind drifting back in time, as she took another sip of coffee. "His name was Derek Manning. He, Colby, and I were actually friends."

"What happened?"

Emmy frowned as the memories wafted through her head. "We were pretty serious about each other for about a year. Then it was time to go off to college, and Derek was determined to go to California. He wanted to work in the tech world. He begged me to go with him."

Dani broke off another piece of her cookie. "But you didn't want to?"

"I had no desire. I'm really quite content in Cape Corral. If I never leave, I'm okay with that."

Dani smiled and nodded. "I see. Those past relationships can make it hard for any future relationships, can't they?"

Emmy tried not to show just how Dani had hit the nail on the head. But she had. Ever since Derek had been in her life, Emmy had no desire to try to make any other relationships work.

Life was purely much simpler when it was just her.

Besides, Emmy wasn't alone. She had her brother, her dad, Colby, and the rest of the island to keep her company.

Most of the time, that thought made her happy.

But for some reason, right now, the idea of finding someone had its appeal.

Maybe it was seeing how happy Levi and Dani were together.

Maybe it was hitting Jeremy on the road and the fear that had ensued.

Maybe it was the anxiety of being trapped in that grave and wondering if anybody would find her in time.

No doubt it was just Emmy's emotions getting the best of her.

The smartest thing she could do was to put it out of her mind.

For good.

―――――

LATER THAT AFTERNOON, Colby asked Emmy to patrol the island with him.

Colby went out once a day to check on the island's wild horses. If any appeared injured or in trouble, the crew developed a plan to help them. Sometimes, that meant intervening medically and pulling the horse out of the wild. Sometimes it meant just monitoring the horse for a while.

Colby and Emmy liked to go horseback riding together quite often. Since the rain had finally broken, Colby had sounded anxious to get out of the station and breathe some fresh air. Emmy couldn't resist joining him. Fresh air sounded great.

Riding a horse was like walking for Emmy. She rarely told people, but she'd been a barrel racing champ when she was in high school. Then she'd decided she didn't like traveling, so she'd given it up. Once she made a decision, there was no changing her mind.

Emmy mounted her horse Butterscotch while

Colby rode Daredevil. Though there was still cloud cover today and the temperature was in the high forties, Emmy found it invigorating. The salty aroma of the ocean always set her soul at ease.

She and Colby made small talk as they started riding on the beach. They'd already passed one harem of horses hanging out by the water. Several other horses were on a nearby dune. The sight never failed to amaze Emmy.

As she glanced at Colby, her heart lurched into her throat.

Lurched into her throat?

Why in the world would it do that? Colby was . . . Colby. Her best friend. Nothing more.

But why hadn't she realized earlier how handsome he was? The man was fit, had a rakish smile that could melt the coldest of hearts, and his eyes were warm and friendly.

He was pretty much . . . perfect.

She shook the thought off, trying to focus on other challenges in front of her. Considering everything that had happened, she really had more important things to focus on.

"Listen, do you mind if we ride past Mr. Henderson's place?" Emmy's mind raced through everything that had happened this week. She desperately wanted answers—especially after being pushed in that grave last night.

Whether she wanted it or not, Emmy was somehow involved in this.

"Mr. Henderson's place?" Colby's forehead wrinkled as he glanced over at her. "Why would we do that?"

Emmy shrugged. "I want to see the other grave that was dug up."

Colby stole another glance at her. "Still thinking about that, huh?"

It was hard *not* to think about. "I can't seem to stop going over everything that's happened. I want to know what someone was looking for."

"I think we all want to know that." Colby clucked his tongue, urging his horse to move faster. "Come on. Let's go."

As they began trotting along the beach, Emmy glanced at the ocean and squinted. Was she seeing things correctly?

"Who is Grant jogging on the beach with?" she asked.

"Abigail Ferguson."

"What? Why would Grant jog with her?" The Fergusons didn't usually associate with the islanders and vice versa.

Guilt plagued Emmy as she said the words, though. It probably wasn't the kindest question, but it felt like lines had been drawn here on the island. People were either enemies of the Fergusons or enemies of the island.

Colby shrugged. "Beats me. I've seen them jogging together a few times. You'd have to ask Grant the answer to that question."

"I'm sure she's nice, it's just that . . . she's a Ferguson." Emmy frowned. Emmy wouldn't admit her true feelings to just anybody, but she'd always been honest with Colby. He knew exactly what Emmy was talking about and wouldn't judge her for the blunt words.

"And the Fergusons *are* sworn mortal enemies of all locals . . ."

Emmy shrugged. "Something like that. It's not right, but the family hasn't done themselves any favors. They haven't exactly tried to fit in or shown any kindness. Mess with me? That's fine. Mess with the horses here? Then you've got trouble."

"That's for sure."

They cut over a sand dune and trotted toward Mr. Henderson's cottage. On the side of his yard was an area where the ground was still mounded and unsettled—the grave that had been dug up.

Colby and Emmy inched closer for a better look.

"Leroy Jones." Colby stared at the headstone. "Why did someone decide to mess with you, Leroy? Your past sins catching up with you?"

Emmy stared at the tattered, worn tombstone. Why had someone messed with him?

"The Jones family still lives on the island," she murmured.

"They do."

An idea hit Emmy . . . one that might be crazy. But what if it wasn't?

"I think we should pay the Jones family a visit."

"But . . ." Colby narrowed his eyes.

She raised an eyebrow. "You have a problem with that?"

"No, not at all."

She smiled. "Okay then. Let's go."

But as they started across the island, her back muscles tightened again.

Emmy glanced around. Was she imagining things? Or was her gut telling her that someone was watching her again?

She glanced around but saw no one. Only houses and a sandy road.

If that was the case, why couldn't she shake this feeling?

As she reviewed everything that had happened, she remembered the cold, hard truth.

She couldn't forget, because this wasn't a nightmare.

This was all too real.

CHAPTER TWENTY-TWO

"I'M SO glad you stopped by, Colby." Jocelyn Jones smiled at him from the doorway of her beachside cottage.

Emmy tried not to grin as she watched the exchange. The woman was obviously smitten with her friend. A lot of single women here on the island were.

Why wouldn't they be? Colby was a catch.

Emmy and Colby had made it all the way over to Jocelyn's place without any incidents. But Emmy had been on edge the whole time, just waiting for more trouble to emerge.

It hadn't.

But that didn't mean she was in the clear.

She halfway expected to see a masked stranger appear again.

If only she could figure out why someone was watching her. Why her address was in the man's pocket. Why the grave behind her house had been dug up.

"Thanks for chatting with us." Colby tipped his hat at Jocelyn, his motions too stiff to be comfortable.

Jocelyn's smile faded as she looked at Emmy. "Good to see you too, Emmy."

Emmy had the distinct feeling Jocelyn didn't care for her—probably because of Colby. A lot of women Colby dated saw Emmy as a threat.

"It's always a pleasure." Emmy offered a smile and a wave. As Jocelyn shut the door, Emmy turned to Colby. "That was a dead end."

"Yes, it was."

Jocelyn hadn't known anything. Mostly, she'd stared at Colby and batted her eyelashes as she'd giggled and responded with exaggeration to every question.

Emmy and Colby climbed back on their horses. Emmy waited until they were away from Jocelyn's house before she said anything.

"At least you got to see Jocelyn." Emmy watched

Colby's expression.

"Jocelyn and I are . . . well, there never was a Jocelyn and me."

"Poor girl. When are you going to tell her you're not interested?"

Colby shrugged. "Like I said earlier, I didn't ask her out again. Doesn't that say it all?"

"Colby . . . you cannot be that dense." Emmy tilted her head.

"What? We went out twice. I didn't make any promises. I don't understand what's so complicated about that."

"You never do." Emmy shook her head, but her eyes danced.

"What does that mean? You look entirely too amused by this." He cast her a skeptical glance as they rode along.

"It means you've left a trail of broken hearts in your path."

"That's hardly true."

Emmy could name off a long list if he needed proof. She didn't. "But it is true. I'm not sure if it's sweet that you don't realize it or disturbing."

"You should go with sweet." He winked.

"You would say that." If Emmy was closer, she might just punch Colby in the arm for trying to be so charming—only because it was working.

"Only because I speak the truth." He clucked his tongue. "Now, I'll race you back to the stable!"

AS COLBY and Emmy raced away from Jocelyn's place on their horses, only one question echoed in Colby's mind.

How could he tell Emmy that the reason none of his relationships worked out was because none of these other women ever measured up to her?

None of them were as funny or kind or beautiful. Not even close.

As Emmy reached The Screen Porch Café first, she flashed a triumphant grin and slowed.

"You won," Colby admitted. "Good job."

"Is it bad that I enjoy beating you?"

"Yes, it's terrible," Colby said. "You should never do it again."

She laughed as they continued walking back to the stable.

A few minutes later, Emmy said, "Brainstorm with me."

Colby's throat went dry as he looked at her. She

was so gorgeous as she bounced in cadence with her horse. She didn't even realize how breathtaking she was . . .

"What other reasons could a person have for digging up graves?" Emmy continued.

"Grave robbers." It seemed like something he'd seen on a Western once.

Emmy cast a skeptical glance his way. "You really think anyone here on the island was buried with anything of value?"

"There is a rumor that pirates lived here at one time. Maybe one of them was buried with their treasure. Maybe it was Blackbeard." He used his most dramatic voice as he offered theories.

"Doubtful. But since there are no bad ideas when we're brainstorming then we'll add it to our list, but . . ."

Emmy was always so kind. She just didn't have a mean bone in her body, did she? Even when she talked about the Fergusons earlier, she'd sounded so sweet while criticizing the family in her own way.

Colby cleared his throat, turning his thoughts back to her question. "Maybe whoever is doing things gets some kind of strange pleasure out of digging up the dead. There are some sickos in the world."

Emmy frowned. "Maybe. But this doesn't feel like that. This person is targeting specific graves."

"Also true." He shrugged. "You know, I really have no idea."

"Whatever's going on, someone was killed for it." Her voice turned soft and wispy as if she mourned someone she didn't even know.

Colby's throat tightened. That was the one detail he couldn't forget.

He wished he could.

But the person behind these crimes wasn't afraid to kill.

Somehow, Emmy was wrapped up in this entire mess . . . a mess involving someone very dangerous.

Colby wished he could pretend Emmy was safe.

He had a feeling she was anything but.

As they started past Emmy's house, Colby sucked in a deep breath.

Levi's truck was parked outside, and the front door was open.

Had something happened while they were gone?

They were about to find out.

CHAPTER TWENTY-THREE

ALARM RACED THROUGH EMMY.

Why was her brother at her house?

She climbed off Butterscotch and tied the horse to one of the posts outside her house. Then she rushed inside, Colby on her heels.

"Levi?" Emmy's gaze went to her brother.

Levi's gaze darkened as he glanced back at her.

Her eyes drifted away from him and scanned the rest of her place. The inside of the inn had been trashed. Photos were off walls, cushions off the couch, and dishes had been smashed.

Her Christmas tree laid on its side and all the stockings had been torn from the mantel.

Emmy gasped as she soaked it all in. "What's going on here?"

"We just got back here, and this is how we found it," Levi explained.

"We?" Emmy's gaze went to Jeremy who stood near the stairway with a frown. "You didn't hear any of this happen?"

"I was with Levi," he explained. "He asked me to come by the station so he could ask a few more questions. When I came back, it was like this. I went and got Levi."

"Why were you needed back at the station?" Concern stained her voice.

"It was nothing," Jeremy said. "We were going over some details about the rental house where I stayed—for insurance purposes mostly."

Emmy stood there a moment, fighting the tears that welled in her eyes as she looked at her house.

Colby placed his hand on her shoulder but said nothing. Instead, he silently offered his support.

"Why would someone do this?" Emmy's voice came out just above a whisper and she rested her hand over her lips, still trying to absorb what happened.

"I'm sorry, Emmy," Levi said. "I checked the rest of your place out. Whoever did this is long gone."

"That's good news, I guess." Her voice didn't sound convincing, even to her own ears.

Her brother turned toward her, his lips tugging down with compassion. "I know you took a lot of time decorating this place and put your heart into it. I'm sorry that someone did this."

Emmy considered herself to be levelheaded. She thought she'd take something like this in stride and be able to see the bigger picture, to focus on the good news that no one had been hurt.

But something about seeing a place that she put so much of herself into destroyed caused a surprising swell of sadness in her.

"I'm just glad no one was hurt," Emmy finally said.

She meant the words. She was glad that Jeremy wasn't here when someone had broken in. Things could have been much worse if he was. She didn't want to see anyone else get hurt.

"What about the bedrooms?" she asked. "Were they destroyed also?"

"They've been gone through, but it will just be a matter of putting things back in place," Levi said. "For now, I need to get Grant and Dash in here so we can look for any fingerprints or other evidence that was left behind. Why don't you guys go hang out at the station for a few minutes while we do that?"

Emmy nodded, though she felt halfway numb inside.

She still couldn't believe that this had happened.

An even bigger question was: how did this connect with the other crimes that had occurred on the island?

ANGER PULSED through Colby when he thought about Emmy's place. Why would someone do this to Emmy, of all people? She was one of the good ones, someone who always looked out for other people. Yet someone had trashed her house.

Not only that, but it made no sense why. It wasn't like Emmy had money or anything of value inside.

Something was definitely going on here.

Colby straightened a picture as he hung it back on the wall.

He had been over at her place helping her to clean up for the past few hours. Dani had also come, along with a few other people here on the island to help. He had a feeling that more people would have come over if the house had been big enough to accommodate everybody.

That's how much people here on the island loved Emmy.

With any luck, they'd hardly be able to tell that anything happened to this place by the time they were done with it. Only a few things had truly been broken—mostly some dishes. Thankfully, the plates had no sentimental value and could be replaced.

As soon as he could catch a moment with Emmy, Colby pulled her into the kitchen. She had looked like she was fighting tears all afternoon, and Colby was anxious to have a moment alone with her.

He pulled her close so nobody could hear. "Are you doing okay?"

Emmy nodded, but the action didn't look convincing. "I'm fine . . . I guess. I'm just . . . confused. I just don't understand why any of this is happening or why someone would have done this."

"It doesn't make much sense, does it?"

"How did someone even get inside?"

"Levi said he saw some evidence that maybe the back lock was picked," Colby said. "That probably makes the most sense."

"Oh Colby . . ."

He drew her into a tight hug, determined that he wouldn't be the one who pulled away. He would wait until Emmy was ready.

As he held her, another surge of anger went through him.

If Colby found the person who'd done this, he'd like to show them a thing or two.

In the distance, he heard Levi's phone ring. Emmy stepped out of Colby's arms and glanced at her brother, her face pinched with anxiety as she waited for an update.

When Levi ended the call, he turned to them. "Good news. That was the county coroner. They think they may have an ID on our John Doe."

"Who is he?" An image of the man flashed through Colby's mind.

"They're going to send the information over in the morning," Levi said. "The coroner still needs to confirm a few things first."

At least that was good news.

They could all use something right now to brighten their day.

CHAPTER TWENTY-FOUR

I'M GETTING CLOSE!

He could feel it in his bones. He'd already gone through that woman's truck. He knew her name. Knew where she lived. And now he was keeping an eye on her place.

He'd seen the woman leave and had followed her for a little while. But trailing her had led to nothing.

That was when he'd decided to go back to the house and look around for himself. Maybe this woman knew something that he didn't. After all, he'd seen her address on that note.

Now he needed to send a message.

He would find what he was looking for, and nobody was going to stop him.

Right now, he sat in the house he'd rented. He

kept the lights off. Kept it dark where no one could see him.

The police were probably out there right now, trying to find whoever had killed that man. Trying to find the person who had trashed that house.

They had no idea that he was sitting right under their noses.

Life had worked out in his favor, and everything had fallen into place. His plan wasn't carefully crafted, yet everything felt like it had been handed to him.

It was almost too easy to get to this point.

He still had a long way to go, he reminded himself. Because Luther had come here for a reason. He knew how to locate something of value.

That woman had something to do with this also.

He was going to keep doing whatever necessary to get what he wanted.

Because nobody was going to take from him what was supposed to be his.

CHAPTER TWENTY-FIVE

THE NEXT MORNING, Emmy paused as she checked her cupboard while making a grocery list.

Jeremy sat at the table with his computer in front of him working on something. He had his ear buds in and didn't appear to hear her. Or maybe he was lost in whatever it was he was writing.

But Emmy's eyes widened when she saw what was on the screen.

A treasure hunt? What in the world was Jeremy researching?

He seemed to realize she was staring and turned around, quickly closing his computer screen. "Emmy! I didn't hear you there."

"I'm sorry. I didn't mean to surprise you. I was just putting some dishes in the hutch."

He shrugged. "I got lost in my story, I guess. That's usually a good sign. This island has inspired me, especially your talk of pirates."

She paused, her curiosity spiked. "Your story is going to have pirates?"

He nodded, his eyes bright with excitement. "And buried treasure too."

"It sounds like it's going to be a winner." Emmy smiled. "Are you feeling okay today?"

"I think I'm getting better and better every day. A lot of that is thanks to you." His gaze seemed to hold sincere gratitude.

"I'm not doing anything. Just giving you a place to stay."

"But it's really so much more than that." Jeremy turned to fully face her. "You've opened up your home and you've served some great food so I don't have to worry about anything. You've been a real lifesaver, Emmy."

He was being so nice but . . . "That means a lot, especially considering that I could have killed you."

He let out a soft chuckle. "I know you feel bad, but please know you shouldn't."

"I do."

He touched her hand. "Emmy, everybody knows

that it was an accident. I should have totally been looking where I was going. If it's anyone's fault, it's mine."

The door opened at the front of the house, and someone stepped inside. Emmy jumped away from Jeremy's touch and turned to see Colby standing there.

Her best friend had slept on her couch again last night but had left this morning to change clothes and then head into work.

Based on the look on his face, he had something that he needed to tell her.

She braced herself for whatever that might be.

She was almost prepared now to receive bad news every time she saw anyone of significance with this investigation.

Emmy hoped this time might be different.

"CAN I HAVE A MOMENT WITH YOU?" Colby tried to keep his instant bad mood at bay. Just because Emmy was talking to Jeremy—and because the man was touching her—didn't mean Colby had to feel jealous.

"Of course." Emmy glanced at Jeremy. "Excuse me a second."

Colby and Emmy stepped outside and onto her porch. As they did, Emmy crossed her arms against the chill outside and made no secret about studying his face.

"You look tired, Colby," she said.

Colby ran a hand over his jaw. "Unfortunately, I didn't sleep well last night. My day isn't going any better yet either."

"What happened?" Her eyes widened with concern as she waited for his response.

"Someone broke into the station last night."

Emmy's eyebrows knit together as a breathless "What?" left her lips.

"It's true. Someone managed to cut the power to the entire place, which rendered our security cameras useless. Once they got inside, they smashed our computers. Levi's over there trying to handle the situation now."

Emmy gasped before shaking her head. "First my place, and now someone is going over to the station to wreak havoc? What sense does that even make?"

"I'd like to know that also."

"Colby . . . I don't even know what to think about

all of this." She rubbed her temple as if she were getting a headache.

Colby licked his lips, knowing that there was one more thing he needed to tell her. It would just be another bit of bad news to an already bad day. But there was no need to keep things secret from her.

Emmy seemed to read his thoughts as she stared at him. "What?"

"I just wanted you to be the first to know that I've been talking to an old friend over the past couple of days."

"Okay . . ."

"He's trying to get me to come work with him up in Norfolk."

She practically gasped. "Up in Norfolk? I don't understand . . . I thought you wanted to stay here in Cape Corral."

Colby squeezed her bicep, seeing the alarm on her face. "I do. But my friend thinks that it would be good for me to get away from this area."

"Why would you say something like that? You love it here." Emmy's voice cracked as if she tried to hold back her emotion.

Colby swallowed hard as he stared at her exquisite face. "I do love it here. But every once in a while, I just think I need a change, you know?"

"I guess . . ." But she still sounded doubtful.

"It doesn't mean that I'm going to take the job."

"But you're thinking about it?"

He shrugged. "I think I'd be foolish not to consider the offer. I love it here . . . but everyone treats me like I'm their little brother. It would be nice to go somewhere where I could be an equal."

"Colby . . ." Emmy tilted her head. "Everyone here loves you."

He stared at Emmy, wishing he could ask if that statement applied to Emmy also. Yet Colby knew that she loved him. But was it in a purely platonic way?

He swallowed hard. The question wouldn't leave his lips.

"I just wanted to let you know so it didn't come as a total surprise later when . . . if . . ." He shrugged again. "You know."

She nibbled on her lip, but Colby could see the frown pulling at the side of her mouth. "Thank you for telling me now. At least I might have some time to prepare myself. The last thing I'd want is for you to take this job and be gone two weeks later."

"I know . . ."

The next instant, Emmy threw her arms around

him in a hug. "Oh, Colby I want you to be happy. I really do. But the thought of you leaving . . ."

Colby held Emmy tight also.

He couldn't imagine leaving her either.

But what if leaving was best for both of them?

CHAPTER TWENTY-SIX

EMMY LEANED back in her bed. She'd escaped to her room to grab a few minutes alone.

She was still trying to comprehend what Colby had told her.

What if he left Cape Corral? She'd never considered the possibility. Colby always seemed so in love with this area, just like Emmy was. She'd assumed her best friend would be here forever.

Emmy couldn't imagine life here without Colby. Without sharing their inside jokes and their game nights and impromptu football games and bonfires. Life on Cape Corral would be markedly grim without her best friend at her side.

But if Colby wanted to leave . . . how could Emmy stop him?

She couldn't.

Just like she hadn't stopped Derek. Emmy had been in love with him, but his desire was to leave and pursue his dreams. His dream wasn't Emmy. That realization had been a tough pill to swallow.

Sometimes Emmy wondered if she still wasn't quite over that insight.

And now Colby . . .?

Her heart squeezed with sadness, and she hugged a pillow to her chest.

Don't think about it right now, Emmy. You shouldn't get ahead of yourself. There's still a good chance that Colby won't take the job and that he'll stay, that things won't change.

She should wait and only start mourning Colby's departure once he actually left.

Right?

Emmy needed to focus on something else, something she could control.

She pulled a notebook from her nightstand and began jotting down the things that had happened on the island. She didn't consider herself an investigator, yet everything that had happened was weighing on her.

Each event was somehow connected to her. Or connected to Colby, and, if something was connected to Colby, then by default it seemed to be connected to Emmy.

As Emmy jotted down her list, her gaze stopped on the two graves that had been dug up.

Those acts had her the most curious.

Why would someone pick those two specific graves to uncover? What sense did it make?

She'd taken a picture of the tombstone near Mr. Henderson's house, and she studied it now.

She and Colby had already talked to Jocelyn, who had no clue about any family secrets concerning the man whose grave had been dug up.

Emmy thought about the disturbed grave in her own backyard. The name on the tombstone was Fletcher Glennis. The Glennis family, as far as she knew, wasn't even on this island anymore.

So what was the connection?

She stared at the information one more time when a thought hit her.

A theory teased her, but she needed to check something out first. Leaving her paper on the bed, she walked out the back door.

She paused by the dug-up grave, which had now been filled back in.

Satisfaction stretched through her as she read the tombstone.

Emmy was right. There was one connection between these two graves. Why hadn't anyone seen this earlier?

Maybe because the tombstone in her own yard was so hard to read. Even in recent years it had become more faded thanks to the elements.

But Emmy had studied these tombstones many times before. So, even as the inscription began to fade, she still remembered some details.

She pulled out her phone and called Colby. "I think I know the connection between these graves that were dug up."

"Please, don't keep me in suspense," he said. "What did you discover?"

COLBY LISTENED to Emmy's theory. She hadn't told him over the phone. She'd wanted him to come to her house. The two of them now sat on the back porch talking.

Emmy had discovered that both of the graves dug up on the island were for people who'd been buried in 1889.

"You're right," he told her. "I'm surprised we

didn't see that earlier. But really, that tombstone is hard to read."

"Do you remember in high school I did that project where I documented all of the graves here on the island?" Emmy asked him.

Colby snapped his fingers. "That's right. I thought that was such an odd project, but you were obsessed with it."

Emmy gave him a playful shove. "Just because you were busy playing football, that did not mean that some of us were not serious about our studies and barrel racing."

He grinned. Seeing Emmy race on her horse had been one of the highlights of his high school years. She was a sight to behold.

She still was.

"I appreciated your passion for the project," Colby said. "If I remember correctly, so did that newspaper out of Raleigh. They did an article on the history of the island and included some of your findings."

"At least someone appreciated it." She raised her chin in mock offense.

"I always appreciate you." Colby grinned. "Do you still have that project?"

"It's somewhere—maybe in one of my old boxes in the attic."

"If these graves keep getting dug up, that might be something we should look for. Maybe we can continue to track this trend and see if it's worth something."

"Good idea."

"But I can't stop wondering why would someone dig up graves from 1889," Colby said. "What sense does that make?"

"I have no idea the answer to that question." Emmy leaned back on her porch swing, her brown hair blowing with the breeze. "But if we can figure that out, then we can figure out why someone is doing this, and possibly even *who* is doing it."

"Do you know what I think we should do?" Colby locked gazes with her.

"What?"

"I think we need to go look for that old research paper."

Emmy grinned. "Let's do it."

CHAPTER TWENTY-SEVEN

TWO HOURS LATER, Emmy and Colby had finally found Emmy's old research paper in a box full of old keepsakes. The two of them sat in Emmy's attic, on the floor, and looked through the paper. They highlighted six different graves she'd listed with the date 1889 on them.

She'd even made a map showing where they were located on the island.

"You were such a nerd," Colby muttered.

Emmy poked him in the ribs and gave him a stern but playful look. "I was smart. There's a difference."

"Is there?"

"I was more like a smart mess."

"Well, if you were a mess, then you make being a mess look very desirable."

Emmy's cheeks heated at his words. Something about the look in Colby's eyes seemed different. Something about it that took her breath away.

Almost as if Colby realized it, he looked away.

That was foolish, Emmy scolded herself. The last thing you need is for Colby to think you have a crush on him or something.

Colby seemed to read her mind and cleared his throat. "What do you say we go look at some of these graves? See if we can find any similarities?"

"Should we tell Levi first?" Emmy tried to imagine her brother's reaction to all this. He'd definitely want to know.

"That's probably a good idea. Then we can help him out. I think having an adventure together sounds like a good idea. It's been awhile."

Emmy smiled. Colby and his adventures. Life was always interesting when he was around. "Yes, it has. Besides, here you are calling me a nerd, but need I remind you that you were with me when I discovered most of these?"

He shrugged. "You know me. I'm always along for the ride."

"And that's just one more thing that I love about you." Emmy's words caught in her throat.

Colby had always been along for the ride.

What if he moved?

She couldn't think like that. And Emmy definitely couldn't let him know how emotional she felt at the thought of him leaving. She didn't want Colby to think that she was trying to sway his decision.

But she could hardly stomach the thought of Colby moving from Cape Corral.

She sucked in a breath and tried to gain control of her emotions before they got the best of her.

"Let me just put on some boots, and let's go," Emmy finally said. "With any luck, we can do this before the next line of showers hit us."

"That's right, they are calling for showers today, aren't they?"

"That's what forecasters say. And they're never wrong."

"No, never." Colby grinned.

Emmy flashed a smile in return.

But, deep down inside, all she could think about was losing her best friend.

COLBY AND EMMY stood near the edge of the town's water tower and took a picture of another tombstone. This was the third one that they'd found that fit their list.

So far, the two of them hadn't discovered anything of note at any of the sites, though.

The winds had picked up, and occasionally some scattered drops would fall. Thankfully, the temperature outside today was nice. And Emmy's company was *always* nice.

As Emmy took another photo, Colby glanced around at the weathered sand dunes. At the sea oats wearing their brown, autumn coats. At Snickerdoodle, one of their wild horses, who stood in the distance staring at them.

Would Colby really be able to leave this place? To leave Emmy?

He wasn't sure. But sometimes he thought the only way he'd ever truly get over Emmy was by not seeing her every day.

Though the thought pained him, maybe it was how Colby could finally move on.

Emmy stepped closer to him and pulled out the map from her back pocket. As she leaned closer, Colby caught a whiff of her apple-pie-scented shampoo.

Not perfume. Emmy wasn't that type.

But she'd always loved her fruity smelling shampoos. The apple-pie scent had been with her since she was probably a preteen.

"Which one should we head to next?" She studied the map, sucking on her bottom lip in that adorable manner she always employed when she was deep in thought.

Colby realized he wasn't thinking about those gravestones at all. He was thinking about Emmy's scent. Thinking about how close she was. Thinking about how much he loved her smile.

He liked to aggravate her just so he could see that playfully stern expression on her face.

That might make him no better than a high schooler with a crush on a classmate, or an elementary student tugging on a girl's pigtail.

Colby wasn't ashamed to admit that he wasn't above those things.

He cleared his throat and tried to return to the present. Emmy had asked him a question.

"How about this one?" He pointed to the closest graveyard on the map, one that was located on the west side of the island, closer to Wash Woods.

"Sounds good." Emmy glanced at the sky. "But

we better go there now before it starts raining harder, right?"

"Makes sense to me. They said we could have more thunderstorms also."

Just as they were about to climb back into Colby's truck, he saw a familiar figure staggering toward them from the beach.

His dad.

Dread pooled in Colby's stomach.

Not now.

Not again.

CHAPTER TWENTY-EIGHT

AS EMMY FELT Colby tense beside her, she followed his gaze and saw his father appear over the sand dune in the distance.

Swallowing hard, she lightly touched Colby's arm. She didn't need to say anything.

Colby knew that she was there for him. She knew how his father always liked to make a mess of things, just when life began to feel normal.

That had been the pattern for Colby's entire life.

Right now, Colby needed to take a deep breath and draw on all his patience.

"Son!" His dad stopped in front of them, his eyes brighter than usual. "It's so good to see you!"

"What are you doing, Dad?" Colby's voice sounded rigid as he stared at his father.

Mr. Morris shrugged, acting like he didn't have a care in the world. "Can't an old man take a walk?"

Colby nodded toward the sky. "It's going to start storming before too long. You should probably make sure you're home first."

His dad waved him off, almost acting giddy. "Oh, I'll be fine. I always am."

Colby stared but said nothing.

The next instant, Mr. Morris reached for Emmy and gave her a quick hug. "If it isn't my daughter-in-law, Emmy!"

"She's not your daughter-in-law, Dad." Colby's voice tightened even more. "She's my friend."

"I thought the two of you were getting married. If you're not, then you should. She's a real catch." His dad wagged his shaggy eyebrows.

"Dad . . ." Some of Colby's irritation seemed to turn to exhaustion.

"It's okay," Emmy assured Colby, placing her hand on his arm. "It's good to see you, Mr. Morris."

He offered a lopsided grin. "It's always good to see you, dear. You're looking as beautiful as ever. Why hasn't my son snatched you up yet?"

"Dad . . ." Colby's voice held warning.

"He never likes to go after what he wants." Mr. Morris widened his eyes as he spouted his views.

"That's why I always tried to teach him to take more initiative. He would never listen to me."

Emmy could sense the tension rising between the men and knew she had to step in before things turned uglier. The last thing they needed was to add another problem to their already long list.

She gripped Colby's arm. "I think Colby is doing a great job. He's one of the reasons this island is so great. He's put out two fires this week alone."

His dad grunted. "Is that right? Maybe those fires shouldn't have been put out. I heard they were at the Fergusons' places. Maybe it would teach them a lesson."

"It pains you that much to give me a compliment, doesn't it?" Colby asked, his muscles bristling.

Tension gripped Emmy's chest muscles until she could hardly breathe. "It's been great seeing you, Mr. Morris. But Colby and I have to go. You give us a call if you decide you need a ride home."

Before Colby could say anything, Emmy tugged him toward the truck. He climbed inside without saying anything, but she could feel the rigidity of his body.

One crisis averted . . . however temporarily that might be.

COLBY FELT the anger coming off him in waves.

His dad almost always had that effect on him.

Thank goodness Emmy had been here. Otherwise, Colby would have probably said something he'd regret.

But his father was just one more reason Colby might need to get off this island.

"You okay?" Emmy's soft voice cut through the air.

Colby put the truck in Drive and pulled down the sandy road. "I guess."

"I'm sorry, Colby. I know your father is a little hard to love at times."

"A little?" He almost snorted. "Sometimes, I feel sorry for him. Mostly, I just don't want anything to do with him."

"I know what he's put you through. I just keep praying he'll turn his life around."

"I think I lost hope a long time ago." Colby shook his head, the motion stiff with years upon years and layer upon layer of emotional history.

"If he changes, it's going to have to be of his own accord," Emmy said. "The one thing that's certain is he has to make the decision for himself. So many people have tried to help him through the years, and they've failed."

"You don't have to tell me that." He tried to turn his thoughts away from his conversation with his dad as "Something to Talk About" by Bonnie Raitt began to play on the radio.

"Colby . . ."

He paused and looked at Emmy. "Yes?"

She turned the radio down as she turned toward him. "I know your dad messes with your head sometimes. But I want you to know that you're one of the most honorable men I know."

His throat tightened at her sincere words. She just looked so earnest, like she didn't doubt a thing she said. "Emmy . . ."

"I mean it, Colby. You're a great friend. You're dependable. You make people laugh. Don't let your dad poison your thoughts."

His heart pounded furiously in his chest. Why did Emmy always know just what to say when he needed to hear it?

The lyrics of the song rushed through him. What would it be like if he and Emmy finally gave people in town something to talk about? If they put an end to the rumors that they were dating—and showed people that they were in love.

But did Emmy love him like that?

Before they could talk more, he stopped at the edge of Wash Woods. Maybe it was better if they were here. Maybe their arrival would stop Colby from saying something he'd regret.

"I think this is the closest we can get to the site," Colby muttered. "We better get moving. We're losing daylight and the opportunity to walk while it's decent weather."

Colby needed to concentrate on other things—like who was digging up graves in the area. Surprisingly, that subject seemed a lot less stressful than thinking about his dad.

CHAPTER TWENTY-NINE

EMMY AND COLBY paused in front of an old cemetery hidden among oaks and beeches, nestled in the reach of holly bushes and under the shade of loblolly pines.

Twelve different tombstones were visible in the brush, many of them crooked and worn down by the elements. But they were proof that at one time past civilizations had thrived in this area. Mostly, the tombstones indicated old sea captains and their families were buried here. There were also rumors that pirates came this way at one time.

Emmy paused in front of the graves and offered a moment of respect to those who had departed.

"Do you see the one we're looking for?" Colby asked.

She scanned the tombstones, double checking with what was on her map.

"It should be that one." She pointed to one on the last row.

She and Colby walked across the briar-filled soil to get closer and to examine the words there.

Sure enough, this was the one they were looking for. The words and numbers were hard to make out, but when Emmy felt along the ridges, this person had clearly passed away in 1889.

The name on the tombstone was Damon Marks, and he had died at fifty-eight years of age.

"This grave isn't disturbed," Colby said. "Is that because someone hasn't found it yet?"

Emmy frowned. "I'd say that is a good possibility. But I'm still not sure what connects these graves other than the date. According to this tombstone, he was a father and friend."

Colby rubbed his jaw, his eyes distant with thought. "You're right. This still doesn't give us a why ... why is someone doing this?"

Just as he said the words, something cracked in the distance.

Colby stepped closer to Emmy as they glanced around, looking for the source of the noise. There were all kinds of wild animals out here. Occasionally, the island's horses came back here also.

But given everything that had happened on the island lately, they needed to make sure that they were safe.

They both remained silent a moment, listening for the sound again.

Before either of them said anything else, a bullet flew through the air.

Someone was shooting at them.

Colby took Emmy's hand and tugged her before yelling, "Run!"

***

COLBY'S HEART pounded into his ribcage.

Someone was shooting at them? What was going on?

All he cared about right now was keeping Emmy safe.

It had been his idea to come out here. He'd never expected anything like this.

Footsteps pounded behind them.

The shooter was chasing them, Colby realized.

If only Colby had brought his gun.

But he hadn't.

They didn't stand a chance trying to stand their ground and fight. Their only choice right now was to run.

Colby kept a tight hold of Emmy's hand as they dodged between trees and tore through thick brush.

Colby didn't know who the gunman was—and he couldn't afford to look back to examine the man's features—but Colby figured that he and Emmy probably knew these woods better than almost anybody on this island.

That gave them an advantage.

But they had to keep moving.

Suddenly, Emmy gasped behind him.

Colby looked back and saw her grab her shoulder.

One of the branches must have cut her.

"Are you okay?" he asked.

She nodded, her eyes wide and her skin turning pale. "Yes, let's keep going. I'll be fine."

Colby was going to have to take her word for it.

Another bullet sliced the air.

If they weren't careful, the gunman would hit one of them next time.

But movement meant life in these situations. The shooter was less likely to hit them if they kept running. It was one of the few lessons Colby's father had taught him.

Just then, thunder clapped overhead and the sky opened up.

The canopy of trees above them stopped the rain —but only slightly.

As they took another step, the sandy ground turned to mud, and Colby and Emmy both began to slide down a steep ridge.

When they stopped at the bottom, he saw the pain on Emmy's face.

She might be athletic, but she wasn't going to make it out here much longer. Emmy's shoulder hurt, she was covered in mud, and her hair was plastered to her face.

They needed to find shelter and call for backup —as soon as Colby knew the gunman was gone.

CHAPTER THIRTY

EMMY TRIED to ignore the pain in her shoulder. A broken tree branch had snagged her shirt and skin. Her hips now ached from her sudden fall.

Maybe sliding down the hill would provide them a chance to get away.

The gunman most likely wouldn't want to follow them this way.

Once at the bottom, Colby pulled her across a small, shallow pond to the other side of the water. They skirted the edge of the pool, rain pelting them with every movement.

Emmy didn't dare look back—it would slow them down too much—but she was desperate to see where the gunman was and what he looked like.

If he was at the top of the hill, he might have a

bird's-eye view of them—perfect for lining up his shot. But the rain shower should obstruct his vision.

Help make us invisible. Please! Emmy muttered the prayer over and over again as Colby continued to pull her to safety.

Thank goodness her best friend was here, acting as her strength when she didn't have any left. Her head swam with emotion and fear—lots of fear—right now.

Colby's grip remained firm on hers as they continued cutting through the dense woods.

Emmy didn't have time to stop and think about the critters out here and the other dangers. She just needed to move, despite how slippery every step was.

Why was someone shooting at them? Had this person followed her and Colby through the woods? Was this about the graves that had been dug up?

She'd have to think about that later.

Colby continued to pull her.

Her body wanted to stop, wanted to rest.

At least no one had fired in several minutes. Maybe they'd lost this guy.

Emmy prayed that was the case.

Just up ahead, an old cabin came into view.

Shelter, Emmy realized.

Just what they needed to keep them safe.

Maybe they could hole up there until help came. The old house would offer protection from this gunman and from the elements.

As far as she was concerned, this place was an answer to prayer.

EMMY AND COLBY ducked into the old cottage as the rain continued to pelt the terrain around them.

"We should be safe here for a while." Colby kept a hand on Emmy's arm, his heart still racing from their escape.

He hadn't seen the man for at least five minutes, and he doubted the shooter would venture down the hillside and across the pond in this weather.

It had been risky, and Colby and Emmy could have easily gotten stuck or hurt.

If Colby had to bet, they'd be safe here until help arrived.

Just in case, he locked the door and placed a chair in front of it to barricade them inside.

The rain pattered on the tin roof above them and the wind caused the building to shake. The whole place smelled earthy, like no one had been inside in years—probably because they hadn't.

Emmy sucked in a deep breath as she turned and looked around the dark cabin. "We've been here before . . ."

Colby stepped closer, a secret thrill of delight rushing through him that she remembered. He hadn't intended on coming here—but this place was one of the few buildings out here in Wash Woods.

"We have," he murmured. "It's an old hunting cabin. I think the Shriver family owns it."

"We came here in high school and played Spin the Bottle."

When there was nothing else to do on the island, people made their own fun. Sometimes, their ideas weren't great. But Colby wasn't complaining about that one.

"You kissed me, and Derek was ticked." Emmy smiled, as if the memory amused her.

"That was the beginning of the end of my friendship with Derek."

Emmy shrugged. "For the record, I always thought he overreacted. He shouldn't have suggested playing the game if he didn't know that was a possibility."

"He used to always tell me to stay away from

you," Colby said, memories of those conversations filling him. "He didn't like the bond we had."

A defiant look flashed in Emmy's gaze. "Well, I think things worked out for the best. Derek left, and here we are."

Colby studied Emmy's face, questions teasing the edge of his mind. He licked his lips before asking, "You still think about him?"

Some of the light left her eyes. "I still remember how much it hurt when he left. I remember how it hurt even more when I heard Derek was in another serious relationship only a month later. It was like our time together meant nothing."

"I know that was hard on you. But not every guy is like him, you know?"

A smile tugged at her lips. "I know."

As she looked away, she reached for her shoulder —where she'd gotten cut earlier.

"What's going on?" Colby murmured.

"I just cut my shoulder when we were running. It's nothing."

Colby narrowed his eyes. "It doesn't look like nothing. You look like you're in pain."

"I'll be okay."

"Let me see your cut," Colby murmured.

Emmy hesitated before turning her shoulder toward him.

When Colby saw the cut there, concern grew in his stomach.

The cut was deep, and he had no first aid kit to clean it.

He needed to think of a backup plan—more than one backup plan, for that matter.

CHAPTER THIRTY-ONE

AS THEY SAT on the couch, Colby put some ointment on Emmy's cut. They'd found an old first aid kit in a cabinet, and he used that to act as a nurse. That was fine by Emmy. She'd never liked blood. But her shoulder hurt, and she knew it needed to be bandaged.

"I don't know what's going on," Emmy murmured as Colby pulled the backing off some bandages. "Why was that man shooting at us? None of the puzzle pieces are fitting."

"I don't like it or understand it either. I especially don't like the fact that you seem to be in the line of fire."

Colby sat close enough that Emmy could feel his body heat. She craved some of that warmth. The rain had soaked her clothes and hair. If they were going to be here much longer, she might even ask him to start a fire—anything to ward away her chills. But hopefully Levi would be here soon. They'd already called him.

He pressed the bandage against her cut before rubbing her stiff back muscles. His hands worked their magic on her, just like they always did.

"You're so good at doing that," Emmy murmured.

"I try. How are you feeling?"

"Better."

He started to pull his hands away.

"No, I mean, it still feels horrible," Emmy murmured, her voice full of teasing. "Keep going."

Colby chuckled. "It's nice to be needed."

"You're always needed, Colby. Always."

As Emmy said the words, lightning flashed outside and thunder clapped.

The sound seemed to remind her of the danger just outside these walls.

The storm was close.

Was the gunman?

Emmy tensed at the thought.

As she did, Colby paused.

She turned around to talk face-to-face. When

Emmy did, she realized their lips were mere inches apart.

She sucked in a breath at how close Colby was.

Yet she couldn't bring herself to pull away. It was much more interesting to study his blue-green eyes. The angle of his cheek bones. His full lips.

Something seemed to sizzle between them in a strange snap of electricity. Colby's hands were on her ... waist? When did his hands go to her waist?

And why was he looking at her like that?

Thunder rumbled again, and Emmy scooted closer.

Neither of them said anything.

Instead, the moment seemed to wrap around them. No words were necessary.

Emmy reached toward him. Her thumb skimmed his jawline before her fingers traveled to the back of his neck. She tugged on the hair there, soaking every inch of him in.

Colby was so familiar to her ... but not this side of him. She'd never touched him like this.

But all she wanted to do was explore. His jaw. His hair.

His lips.

His lips? This was Colby. What was she thinking?

She had no idea.

Rain continued to pound overhead, the cadence matching the thrum of her heart.

Her gaze went to Colby's lips again, and Emmy remembered that kiss they'd shared during Spin the Bottle. It was the only time they'd ever kissed.

Back then it had been awkward. She'd been dating Derek. Colby had been her best friend, the boy who chased her around with snakes, who explored ditches looking for tadpoles, and who had been her partner in crime.

Right now, Emmy ran her thumb across his jaw.

Colby's jaw.

Her Colby.

That's how it had always felt, at least.

The next instant, his lips covered hers. He hesitated only a moment—as if waiting for her to rebel—before his mouth consumed hers.

Emmy wrapped her arms around his neck and held on, breathless as she thought about kissing him more. Because she wasn't ready for this to end. His lips pulled and tugged and explored in all the right ways.

Suddenly, a knock sounded behind them.

Emmy flinched and shot away from Colby, hardly able to breathe.

What had just happened?

Her lips still felt swollen. Her heart raced. Her arms craved feeling Colby against her again.

Which was crazy.

Colby looked just as dazed as she did.

She opened her mouth, trying to find the words.

Before she could, the knock sounded again.

"Emmy? Colby? Are you there?"

Levi.

He'd gotten here surprisingly quick.

Emmy swallowed hard, nearly grateful for the distraction. She needed to sort out her thoughts about what had just happened.

Because her whole world just felt like it had been turned upside down.

She'd just kissed her best friend.

And she wanted to do it again . . . and again.

***

HAD Emmy felt the same fireworks exploding between them as he did?

Based on her wide-eyed, breathless reaction, Colby would definitely say yes.

That kiss . . . it had been more than he had ever dreamed it would be. The two of them together . . . they just felt right. Like they belonged.

And Emmy's lips . . . they felt amazing against his. All he wanted to do was to explore them more. To smell her apple scent again. To know that the same heat he felt, Emmy felt also.

Instead, Levi stood in the cottage doorway and stared at them. "Are you two okay?"

"We got in just before the storm got worse." Emmy's voice sounded scratchier than usual as she stared at her brother.

Levi's gaze went back and forth between the two of them. "You guys seem off. Are you sure you're okay?"

Colby nodded. "Just waiting for you to show up. Thanks for coming."

Levi nodded toward the woods behind him. "I didn't see anyone out there. Whoever chased you must be long gone."

"That's good news," Emmy muttered, rubbing her hands over her arms as if chilled.

"We can talk more back at the station," Levi said. "Let's get you out of here before the storm gets worse."

Colby glanced at Emmy once more. As he did, she stole a glance at him also.

Colby saw the shock still on her features.

Emmy hadn't expected that, had she?

Neither had he.

The moment had just seemed right. And Emmy had looked so beautiful, so alluring.

She *was* so beautiful—inside and out.

But they needed to talk about what had just happened.

That wouldn't be happening right now.

First, they needed to figure out this gunman.

Their lives depended on it.

CHAPTER THIRTY-TWO

EMMY ALMOST FELT like she was in a daze as she sat at the station with some dry clothes on and a cup of coffee in hand. She and Colby had gone through all the details of what had happened—minus the kiss—with Levi. Her brother had taken notes with that concerned expression on his face.

"I don't like this," he said when they were done. He leaned back in his chair, a contemplative expression on his face.

"Neither do we," Colby muttered. "Whoever fired that gun must have been following us."

"But why shoot at you?" Levi narrowed his eyes. "You may have led this person to the grave he was looking for. It doesn't make sense though why he would fire."

"I don't understand it either." Emmy shrugged.

Levi shook his head before letting out a sigh. "I'm going to have one of my guys monitor those graves. If these people really are trying to dig up graves from 1889, then we want to be there when they come back to finish the task. Maybe we'll get some answers then."

"With any luck, maybe this person will be caught," Colby said.

"I'm just glad that the two of you are okay," Levi said. "Things could have turned out a lot differently."

Emmy shivered and nodded as she sat there.

"Colby, there are a few things that I could use your help with here if you don't mind," Levi said.

Colby stole a glance at Emmy. No doubt Levi wanted to talk about what just happened. But Emmy was glad to have a little space. She needed to sort out her jumbled thoughts—about a lot of things, not just being shot at.

"I can walk myself back to the inn," Emmy said. "It's no problem."

"I'd say you shouldn't be there alone with your visitor, but he has been sitting on the porch for most of the day, so I know he wasn't the one behind that gunfire." Levi narrowed his gaze again. "But I would still like for you to keep your doors locked and call me if you have even the smallest suspicion that something is wrong."

Emmy rose to her feet. "Of course."

She stole one more glance at Colby. The look in his eyes was different than usual. There was something warm and burning there, as if their unspoken conversation haunted him.

They did need to talk. But she wasn't sure what to tell him.

Emmy swallowed hard and offered a nod. "I'll be in touch with you two later."

She scrambled from the room.

She had a lot to think about.

"How about if I walk you back, just to be safe?" Colby offered.

"Sure." Emmy couldn't deny the rush of nerves that went through her at the thought of being alone with him again.

She couldn't stop thinking about that kiss. About his lips against hers. About how . . . how something felt like it could be changing between them.

They walked silently for the first few minutes back to her place. But Emmy knew that there were things that needed to be said between them.

She was certain that Colby felt the same way.

They paused on her porch, and Emmy turned toward him. She shoved her hands into her pockets, figuring they were safer there. The last thing she needed was to reach for him again.

If she did, they could end up in another lip lock.

She cleared her throat, trying to ward away the thought. "We should probably talk about what happened."

Colby stepped closer. "We probably should."

At once, panic rushed through her. Colby was her best friend. There was no place for romance in their relationship. What if he hadn't felt the same spark? What if this messed up the good thing they had going?

Even worse—what if that kiss drove Colby away from this island?

"I think we can both agree that it was a mistake," Emmy said. "We were both just caught up in the moment and ..."

Colby's face almost seemed stoic as he stared at her. Finally, he nodded. "Of course. I was going to say the same thing. It was a ... mistake."

Relief—and disappointment—flushed through her. "We could just pretend it didn't happen and go on?"

Colby swallowed hard, hard enough that she saw

his Adam's apple bob up and down. "You took the words right out of my mouth. It never happened."

Emmy nodded, even though the motion felt stiff. "Then it's settled. We will erase that moment from our minds."

He opened his mouth as if to say something else before finally nodding again and taking a step back. "Now that that's settled, I should get back. I'll check on you later."

"That sounds great."

But as Emmy watched him walk away, her heart flip-flopped.

What exactly was going on inside her?

I THINK we can both agree that it was a mistake.

Emmy's words echoed in Colby's mind as he walked back to the station.

Of *course* that hadn't been what he was going to say. Yet, after Emmy's declaration, Colby couldn't force out the words he'd planned to share.

Sadness pressed on him at the thought. Colby had thought there for a moment that something wonderful had developed between them. That maybe the two of them actually stood a chance.

Colby should have known better though.

What would have happened back there if he'd actually told the truth? If he had admitted his feelings to Emmy?

He'd thought about doing so but had changed his mind. Emmy was willing to put that kiss behind them. Colby should back out now before he got in so deep that their relationship was forever damaged.

He wandered into the stable where Levi held a clipboard as he checked their supplies for the horses. Everyone at the station helped take care of the horses here on the island. Colby grabbed a pitchfork so he could clean out the stalls.

"You seem distracted," Levi muttered as he looked at the horse feed.

Colby looked up at the sound of Levi's voice. "Do I? Sorry."

"Why don't you just tell my sister that you like her?" Levi said as he marked things off on a list in his hands.

Colby paused and then stabbed the pitchfork into the ground. He started to argue at the statement but then changed his mind. There was no need to deny his feelings anymore. It was clear to everybody but Emmy that Colby had feelings for her.

He shrugged. "Maybe I will."

"It will have taken you long enough." Levi's eyebrows flicked up before continuing looking through their supplies.

"If I tell Emmy how I feel, and she doesn't share those feelings . . . then things will never be the same between us." It felt good to be honest, to not hide the truth anymore. He'd been hiding it for too long.

"But if you don't tell her, what if there could have been something great between the two of you that changed the course of your life?"

"That's easy for you to say," Colby said. "You're happily married."

"I am. And I'm so glad that I found Dani. She makes my life better."

"Emmy makes my life better, whether that's as a friend or something more."

Levi stared at him a moment longer before finally nodding, seeming to sense that Colby was ready for a subject change.

"So, what do you think is going on here in this town?" Levi asked.

Colby let out a long breath. "I wish I knew. I keep trying to connect each of the incidents that have happened here on the island, but I can't seem to piece them together."

"It is odd, isn't it?"

"The only thing I can figure is that somebody is trying to dig up graves for some reason. Maybe this guy whose body we found tried to get in this person's way?"

"That's the only thing I can think of as well."

"Did you ever get that report on our dead man's identity?" Colby asked.

"I've been trying to download it on my phone, but the files are too large. Our computers should be up and running here soon. When they are, we'll know more. Hopefully, that information will help us find some answers then."

"I don't suppose there have been any leads on these arsons, have there?" Colby thought he would have heard from Dillon, but he hadn't.

"You know how hard it is to track down arsonists. Any evidence that was left, burned up. Nobody saw anything. Trying to track down anybody who made huge accelerant sales has proven futile as well. There's just really not that much to go on."

"Are the Fergusons still ticked at us?"

"You better believe it." Levi nearly snorted as he shook his head. "They are holding this whole town personally responsible."

Colby shook his head. "Some people. By the way, what's the update on that situation? Anything?"

"There's a bidding war going on right now on some property here," Levi said. "The Fergusons keep bidding and then Dash's nonprofit bids at a higher rate. But the Fergusons' plan to build has been tied up with the county. I'm hoping that nothing will come of it, but we all know that money can talk."

Colby frowned. "Yes, it can."

"The good news is that the flood water is finally starting to recede," Levi said. "The nor'easter is pulling offshore. They're hoping to open the clinic back up in a couple of days even."

"I'll take whatever good news you've got to offer."

Just then, Levi's phone buzzed. He glanced at the screen. "It looks like we have an ID on our John Doe."

Colby stepped closer. "Who is he?"

Levi glanced up. "Isn't this interesting . . ."

Colby's interest piqued as he waited to hear what Levi had learned.

CHAPTER THIRTY-THREE

EMMY COULDN'T STOP THINKING about that kiss with Colby. Her lips still tingled. She wanted to feel the hardness of Colby's chest beneath her hands. To feel his hair at the tip of her fingers.

Where in the world were these thoughts coming from?

She tried to put them all out of her mind as she furiously cleaned the kitchen. She'd found an old toothbrush and used it to scrub the grout around the kitchen sink and faucet. Somehow, the act helped her get some energy out.

Her guest was upstairs in his room, so Emmy enjoyed a moment of reflective quiet.

But only one question lingered in her head.

What if she *was* ready to date? All these years,

she'd assumed she just wanted to stay single. But had she assumed that out of fear?

Emmy had always attributed that goal to the fact that she wanted to be like the wild horses on the island. But even those wild horses weren't destined to be alone. Could she still be free while in a relationship?

She hadn't asked those questions in a long time. But seeing how happy her brother was now that he was with Dani had begun to soften her heart. Then her friend Dash had met Lizzie. Even Fire Chief Dillon McGrath had fallen in love and gotten married recently.

And the thing was, their lives seemed better for it. Not worse.

Just because Derek had broken her heart, that didn't mean that Emmy should never give love a try again. She knew good and well that it might mean her heart would be broken again.

But maybe love was a risk worth taking.

She heard a footstep behind her and turned. Jeremy stood there with a smile on his face as he lifted his laptop in his hand. "Didn't mean to scare you. I was going to sit on the back porch and write for a little while."

"You'll have to excuse me"—she paused with a

toothbrush in her hands as she scrubbed the sink—
"I'm just jumpy today."

"There's no problem." He leaned against the wall as if in no hurry to start writing.

"Can I get you something to drink?" Emmy drew in a breath, trying to collect herself.

"Actually, I'm glad I ran into you," Jeremy started. "Emmy, you've been so kind to me. I wondered if I might do something nice for you in return. How would you feel about going out to grab some dinner tonight?"

"Dinner?" Emmy repeated trying to buy some time.

She'd just given herself a pep talk about dating. And it wasn't necessarily that Jeremy was asking her out on a date. But this seemed like a logical first step.

Besides, Emmy couldn't say anything bad about this man. He'd been nothing but polite since he arrived. Levi had even said Jeremy had been on the porch all day today, so it wasn't like he was behind any of the crimes happening here on the island.

After thinking about it for another moment, Emmy finally nodded. "Sure. Some dinner together would be nice."

Why not? She needed to open herself up to

dating. And Jeremy was an attractive, intelligent man.

"HOW CAN our dead man's name possibly be Jeremy Riesling?" Colby repeated as Levi stood in front of him, staring at his phone. "Jeremy Riesling is the man who's staying at the inn with Emmy."

Levi shook his head and lowered his cell. "That's what I'd like to know also. All the information is the same . . . where this guy said he was from and what he did for a living. But his picture is clearly not Jeremy's."

"How certain is the person who sent you this information?"

"It's not foolproof. Officials are going off a photo identification. Our dead man had no fingerprints on file. We'll double check the dental records, but that will take more time."

"I don't like this." Colby rubbed his jaw, feeling it tighten as he leaned against the stable wall.

Levi let out a long breath. "I don't either. It looks like I need to go have a chat with this guy."

"You mind if I go too?"

"Why not?" Levi shrugged.

They left their equipment in the stable and strode next door to the inn.

As Colby got closer, he saw Emmy and Jeremy laughing through the window. He felt himself bristle at the sight.

He didn't want to be jealous of the man, but he couldn't deny that Emmy almost seemed to be drawn toward her guest. Now there was this mix up . . . or whatever it was.

Either way, Colby had a bad feeling about the man from the start.

Levi knocked at the door before opening it. Emmy strode across the room toward them, but her smile faded as if she knew something was wrong as soon as she saw her brother's face.

"We need to have a word with Jeremy," Levi said.

Emmy's face lost some of its brightness as she extended her arm behind her. "Of course. Come in."

Colby felt another rush of attraction as he stepped past Emmy.

Did she feel it too?

Based on their earlier conversation, he'd say no.

This wasn't the time to think about that—yet it was all Colby could think about.

Levi strode across the room toward Jeremy, who stood near the back door with his laptop in his hands. "Some new information has come to light, and we have a few questions for you."

"Of course." Jeremy straightened.

Levi pointed to the table. "Have a seat at the table. Please."

Levi's "please" made it clear it wasn't a request. His voice was interrogator hard.

Jeremy shrugged, his gaze shifted as if he were nervous—as anyone would be in this situation. But he did as Levi instructed.

Colby remained in the background, watching everything happen and standing guard, just in case things went wrong. Emmy remained close to him, and she rubbed her hands together as if nervous.

He couldn't imagine what this guy was about to say. What possible excuse could Jeremy have for this? Had he stolen a dead man's identity?

"I'm going to need to see your ID," Levi started.

"Sure. Of course." Jeremy reached into his pocket and pulled out his wallet. A moment later, he slid his driver's license across the table.

Colby wasn't close enough to see the picture there, but he waited anxiously for Levi's reaction.

Levi's face remained placid as he jotted a few things down before pushing the license back over to Jeremy.

"Your name is Jeremy Riesling," Levi said.

"Correct."

"You're thirty-two years old."

"Also correct."

"Where are you from?"

"Newport, New Hampshire." Jeremy shifted. "What's this about?"

Levi's jaw hardened. "A man was found dead here on the island earlier this week. We just got the information back on his identity. His real name is Jeremy Riesling."

Emmy gasped beside Colby, and her hand flew over her mouth.

Jeremy shook his head, confusion crossing his gaze as if he had no idea what Levi was talking about.

"That makes no sense," Jeremy muttered. "Why would he be using my name?"

"That's what we're trying to figure out," Levi said. "Your driver's license clearly indicates that you are Jeremy Riesling. Something fishy is going on here."

CHAPTER THIRTY-FOUR

COLBY CAREFULLY WATCHED Jeremy's expression as he processed that news. The man shook his head before pinching the skin between his eyes.

"I don't understand," Jeremy said. "That doesn't make any sense. Could this man have followed me here and tried to steal my identity?"

"Why would he do that?" Levi narrowed his eyes with discernment.

"That's what I would like to know also."

"Have you ever seen the man before?" Levi pulled out his phone and held up a picture.

Colby watched Jeremy's expression carefully, looking for any sign of recognition in the man's eyes. Instead, Jeremy blanched, as if seeing the lifeless body shook him up.

"Now that you mention it, he might look a little familiar." Jeremy shook his head, his gaze fastened to Levi's phone. "I don't know why though. I'm not sure exactly that I can place him."

"Give it a minute," Levi murmured.

Jeremy let out a long breath and hung his head. A moment later, he looked up and realization stretched through his gaze. "There was a man who kind of looked like him who attended a writers' group I was at. Now that you mention it, I did run into that same man at the grocery store a few days later. I assumed it was a coincidence . . ."

"So you think this man may have been obsessed with you and followed you here?"

Jeremy shrugged and ran a hand through his thick, dark hair. "I'm not saying anything. I'm just throwing it out there."

"I'm still not sure what sense it would make for him to steal your identity," Levi said.

"I wish I could help you out. I wish I had answers. But I'm just as confused as you are. I have no idea what's going on here."

"Do you think there are people out there who might think you have clout because you're a screenwriter?" Levi asked. "Could someone want to imitate you to try to get some type of potential benefit from pretending to be somebody that he wasn't?"

"I suppose it's a possibility. But it would have been a better possibility if I was a successful screen-writer, which I am not."

"I've seen people obsess over less." Levi shrugged, looking noncommittal as to his opinion. "We're going to keep looking into this, but thank you for your time. If I have any more questions, I'll be sure to be in touch."

Jeremy nodded. "That sounds good. Thank you for all your hard work. It means a lot."

"And we'd like it if you remained on the island while the case is ongoing."

"Of course. I have no plans to leave any time soon."

With that, Levi stood, nodded toward Jeremy, and then walked toward Colby. "We better get back."

Colby gave one last lingering glance at Emmy before stepping out.

There was so much he wanted to say to her.

But maybe he'd already said too much.

EMMY FELT an unexpected rush of nerves after that conversation. She wrapped her arms across her chest as she turned to Jeremy.

Swallowing the lump in her throat, she said, "That was surprising, huh?"

He shook his head and quickly rubbed his temples as he slumped at the kitchen table. "You can say that again. I didn't see that curveball coming, that's for sure."

Emmy sat at the table across from Jeremy. "So, you think that man might have been familiar?"

She was trying to put everything she'd learned together, but this was going to take a while to process.

Jeremy shrugged and shook his head again. "Like I said, the man does vaguely look like someone who came to a writers' group one time. And I do believe I saw him in a store after that, but I didn't think much of it. I certainly didn't think that the man might steal my identity and follow me to this island."

"That does seem like a pretty desperate thing to do. I mean, if this man was obsessed with you, maybe I could see him wanting to follow you. But stealing your identity? It takes it to a whole entirely different level." The thought left Emmy feeling unsettled.

"You're telling me." Jeremy shook his head again before seeming to clear his thoughts. "Are you still good for dinner tonight or do you want to postpone? Either way, I'm starving."

Emmy considered his question for only a minute. Why not eat together? How could that hurt anything? She wasn't committing to a relationship.

She was simply being social.

Finally, she nodded. "Dinner tonight still sounds good. You do realize there's only one restaurant here on the island though, right?"

Jeremy smiled. "It doesn't really matter where we go to eat. I just want to have a chance to get to know you a little bit better."

Emmy felt the heat rising in her cheeks. She was so out of practice when it came to dating. "When would you like to leave?"

He stood. "Can you give me a few minutes to go get cleaned up?"

"Of course. I'd like to get cleaned up also. As you could probably guess, the restaurant here is very casual."

He grinned again before stepping toward the stairs. "I am okay with casual."

"Good. Then I'll see you in a few."

With that thought, Emmy disappeared into her room.

She was surprisingly nervous as she changed. But maybe that was because she hadn't been on a date in a very long time.

She hoped she didn't regret this.

The kiss she and Colby had shared floated through her mind.

In some ways, she already did.

CHAPTER THIRTY-FIVE

COLBY AND LEVI stopped by the stable before heading toward the station beside it. Before Colby stepped inside, he paused. "If you don't mind, Levi, I need to go back and tell Emmy something."

Levi raised his eyebrows. "Of course. Good luck, man."

It was like his friend knew what he was about to do without Colby saying anything.

But there was no more time to waste. Colby had put this off for far too long.

He needed to tell Emmy that their kiss wasn't a mistake, that he didn't regret it, and that he had wanted to do it for such a long time.

Colby had no idea how she would respond. But he didn't want to keep that inside him any longer.

He hurried across the sand and pounded on her door. A moment later, Emmy pulled it open and her eyes widened. She'd cleaned up already, and her hair fell in clean waves around her face. She'd pulled on a dark blue shirt and her favorite jeans.

"Colby." Surprise captured her voice. "You're back again."

"Can we talk?" he rushed.

Her gaze turned serious as she nodded. "Of course. Is everything okay?"

"I'm hoping that it will be." Colby's heart pounded into his ribcage. But he wasn't backing down now. "There's something I need to tell you, Emmy."

"You know that you can tell me anything, Colby."

He swallowed hard before taking off his cowboy hat and placing it over his chest. "Good. I'm hoping you mean that. Because when I kissed you today, Emmy . . . I don't regret a moment of it. I don't think it was a mistake. And all I want to do is to kiss you like that again."

Her eyes widened. "What? Colby . . ."

"Don't say anything. Not yet. I just need to get this out." He drew in a deep breath. "I have loved you since second grade, Emmy Sutherland. The only reason none of my other relationships last is because

I compare every girl to you, and nobody else measures up. You make me a better man and a better person, and the thought of you not being in my future makes it seem considerably dimmer."

She smiled and tilted her head to the side, as if she thought his words were sweet.

"I know you don't have any interest in dating," Colby continued. "I know that you're happy being single. But I'm hoping that maybe somewhere down the line you might consider the idea that you'd be even happier if you did date, as long as it was the right person."

"Colby . . ." Emmy frowned, something akin to panic filtering through her gaze.

Colby had to finish, so he charged ahead before he could chicken out. "I've never wanted to tell you this because I didn't want to ruin our friendship. It means the world to me. But I've also realized that I've wasted so much time, and time isn't something that we're guaranteed. I'm hoping that when we kissed earlier that you felt the same fireworks I did."

Colby paused and stared at Emmy as she stared back at him. He couldn't read her expression and had no idea what she was thinking.

"I think I'm done." He shoved his hands in his

pockets, suddenly feeling panicked. What was Emmy going to say? How would she react?

As she licked her lips and looked up at him, Colby braced himself for her response.

EMMY'S MIND REELED. Had Colby really just admitted that he loved her? Loved her as more than a friend?

It would take a while for those words to settle in her mind.

But Emmy knew part of her loved Colby too. She'd felt those fireworks.

But above that, part of her was afraid—afraid their friendship would be ruined. Afraid that Colby would break her heart like Derek did.

She was trying to take baby steps and maybe consider the idea of dating again.

But Emmy hadn't expected this.

As she stared up at Colby now, she licked her lips, unsure exactly what to say.

Part of her wanted to say yes, that she more than anything wanted to jump into a relationship with him. But the other part of her held back, afraid to make that commitment.

"I am a little speechless right now," she finally started.

"Is that a good speechless or a bad speechless?" Colby tilted his head, hope filling his gaze.

Emmy wasn't sure how to answer because the last thing she wanted to do was to give him reason to lose faith. "Colby, I—"

Before she could say anything else, the door behind her opened and Jeremy stepped out. "Are you ready to have dinner?"

Emmy's gaze shot to Colby, and she saw his smile disappear.

Remorse filled her, churning in her gut until she felt like she might throw up.

What awful timing.

"The two of you are having dinner?" Colby's words sounded stiff.

Jeremy lightly touched her back and chuckled. "I know. I can't believe she said yes either."

Colby's gaze shot back to hers. "I see." He placed his cowboy hat back on his head. "Well, I wouldn't want anything to stop the two of you."

Emmy opened her mouth to say something else, but the words wouldn't leave her lips. She still wasn't sure exactly what she wanted to say.

Before she could figure it out, Colby offered a

quick wave before stepping off the porch.

Emmy watched him leave, sadness welling inside her. Her heart felt like it was being pulled in two, and she desperately wanted to reach out to him.

Jeremy stepped closer, following Colby's departing figure with his gaze. "I hope I didn't interrupt anything . . ."

Emmy glanced at him and attempted a smile. But she knew the expression didn't reach her eyes.

Her whole world felt like it had just been turned upside down, and she had no idea what to do about it.

CHAPTER THIRTY-SIX

COLBY STORMED BACK into the station, desperate for a moment alone. Irritation simmered in him, and he didn't want to blow. He just needed to make it back to his office.

Just as he stepped inside, Levi stepped from the reception area and observed him.

"You did it, didn't you?" Levi's voice sounded low and serious.

Colby scowled as he continued toward his office. "I don't want to talk about it."

Despite his words, Levi trailed behind him. "I take it things didn't go well?"

"Turns out Emmy's going on a date with her house guest." His throat tightened as he said the words.

"Jeremy?" Levi's gaze darkened. "That doesn't sound like Emmy. She hates dating."

"Believe me, she's definitely going on the date. And I think she's excited about it."

"I wish she would have at least waited until we found out some more information about this guy." Levi's voice held the same doubt that Colby felt building inside him.

"You and me both." Colby reached his office and sat down in his chair harder than he'd intended.

Levi lingered in the doorway. "I'm sorry it didn't go the way you wanted it to. I know Emmy cares about you."

Colby scowled. "On a platonic level."

"You don't know that. Maybe she just needs some time to let this all sink in."

"Maybe." He offered a stiff shrug.

Right now, all Colby felt was regret. He should never have told Emmy how he felt.

Even worse, what if their kiss had awakened something inside her? But what if it had awakened something that *didn't* include Colby? Maybe that kiss had made Emmy realize that she did want more than just staying single—just not with him.

In fact, Emmy might think of Colby as an older brother.

His stomach knotted at the thought of it.

"Give her some time," Levi encouraged. "I don't see that Jeremy guy as being her type anyway."

"But relationships surprise us all the time now, don't they?" Colby had seen it enough times before—people falling in love with someone no one expected.

Levi shrugged. "I'll be praying for you, Colby. Don't give up. Not yet."

As he said the words, the alarm sounded at the station.

Colby hopped to his feet.

It looked like they had another fire to attend to.

"HOW IS it that someone like you is still single?" Jeremy asked over his crab cake sandwich. "I know it sounds like a line, but I didn't intend it that way. I really do want to know."

Emmy shrugged and picked at the fish nachos she'd ordered. Her appetite was pretty much gone, and she couldn't stop replaying Colby's words.

It was more than his words she recalled. It was the devastated look in Colby's eyes when he'd seen Jeremy step out for their dinner date.

Part of her wished she'd had time to explain.

The other part of her was grateful for a little extra time to process what Colby had said.

Could Emmy really love Colby in a romantic way? Was that a possibility?

She didn't know. It was a big step.

Emmy had figured that going out with Jeremy would be a good start to jumping back in the social scene. The man probably wouldn't be around for that long. Going out with him would kind of help her get her feet wet, so to speak.

Then why was she sitting across from Jeremy but thinking of Colby?

The last thing she wanted was to make an emotional decision, to jump into a relationship with Colby only because their feelings were so heightened after everything that happened this week. If she wasn't certain about her choice, then the aftermath could change her future.

How would she and Colby take steps backward? Could they?

Or would exploring a relationship that might not work between them ruin their friendship? Would she only end up with a shattered heart? After all, Emmy had the reputation for not wanting to settle down. But Colby was the one who'd seemed unable to commit to anyone he'd dated over the past ten years.

Emmy cleared her throat, her thoughts drifting back to the present. "I've been very happy by myself for a long time. I determined early on that I didn't need a man to make me happy in life, but that I was going to make my own happiness."

Jeremy's eyes glimmered with curiosity. "Do you still feel that way?"

She shrugged again. "I don't know what to say. But maybe God is softening my heart and making me realize that it's okay for things to change. Maybe I should be more open-minded to what my future might look like."

"That realization only makes you more fascinating." Jeremy grinned before he took another bite of his sandwich.

"How is your screenplay going?" The question seemed inconsequential when Emmy considered everything that had happened, but she was determined to make some small talk and distract herself. . . for a little while, at least.

"It's going okay. I've really found a lot of inspiration on this island, so that's a good thing—a really good thing."

"That is a good thing. I think this place is great."

"You're not the only one. I think it's absolutely fascinating. So while I'm sorry that you hit me, I am glad we were able to meet." Jeremy flashed another grin. "You've been a great resource as to what life is like here on this island. Between the cemetery in your backyard, the feral cat colony, and these wild horses that roam everywhere . . . I almost feel like I stepped into a whole different world."

"And that's what's so great about Cape Corral, isn't it?"

"Yes, it is." Jeremy's grin slipped. "Did I hear you were out looking for gravesites earlier? I wasn't trying to eavesdrop—but the walls can be thin in the house."

"I did go out looking for some, mostly just out of curiosity."

"How did that go, if you don't mind me asking?"

Emmy remembered the gunfire, remembered running through the woods, and remembered finding shelter as the storm raged outside.

She repressed a shiver. "Colby and I didn't discover anything."

"It was a good try."

"There are a few new cemeteries that have been uncovered since I wrote my paper. Maybe someone will check those out also."

"Seems like someone should look."

Emmy swallowed hard at the reminder of everything that had happened.

Before she could respond, she glanced out the window. A man ducked into a truck across the street.

Her breath caught.

Was that the man who'd been watching her?

As the truck sped away, Emmy knew that it was.

But she hadn't caught a glimpse of the man.

She only knew he was dangerous.

And that he was still watching her.

TWO HOURS LATER, another fire on one of the Fergusons properties had been extinguished.

Just as with the others, this fire appeared to have started in a backroom using some kind of accelerant. Dillon and Colby hadn't been able to examine the scene thoroughly yet, but no one had any doubt that this was another strike by the arsonist.

Colby and Dillon, along with the volunteer firefighters and the crew from the forestry service, stood outside the house now. The scent of smoke lingered in the air and water from the hoses puddled on the ground. Crowds had gathered in clusters around the scene.

Levi went around talking to any potential

witnesses. This was the first fire that had occurred in broad daylight. That made the chances of someone seeing something a little more likely.

Most of the massive house had been salvaged. But it was becoming clearer that they had to find the person responsible for these fires before someone got hurt.

Thankfully, many of these homes were vacation homes and full-time residents didn't live in them, especially in the cold winter months. But that didn't mean that things couldn't turn ugly one of these days.

As Colby waited for the structure to cool, he spotted Mr. Ferguson pulling up in his truck. The man threw the vehicle into Park before storming across the sand toward Levi.

"I'm beginning to think that you are incompetent," the man seethed. "If this was happening with one of your locals, the arsonist would have been found by now."

Tension stretched across Levi's face, but he remained cool. "I assure you that my guys and I are doing everything possible to find the person responsible. It isn't a crime we take lightly."

Mr. Ferguson's gaze darkened. "You couldn't

prove that by me. One of these days, someone is going to get hurt."

Levi swallowed hard before asking, "Sir, do you have security cameras set up in any of your houses?"

"Of course. But some were burned with the fires, so there was nothing on them."

"What about this house?" Levi nodded at the latest casualty.

"I can check for you."

"You do that. In fact, if it's okay, I'll accompany you so we can check together."

Mr. Ferguson's gaze darkened. "I don't see why you need to accompany me, but if that's what you have to do, then come on."

As Colby continued to stare at the charred remains of the house in the distance, he couldn't help but think that it reflected a bit of his relationship with Emmy.

Their bond had once been beautiful and strong, but now it started to smolder away to the bare bones. The question was, would the two of them rebuild or would they let the remains wither away with the elements?

Someone tapped him on the shoulder.

Colby turned to see Abigail Ferguson standing there with a frown on her face.

"There's something I need to tell you," she said.

His eyes narrowed. "What's going on?"

"I thought you should know . . . I saw your father by this house earlier. He had a bottle of alcohol with him."

Colby bristled. "Did you see him go inside?"

Abigail hesitated before nodding. "That's how it looked."

Colby let that thought race through his mind.

Could his dad be the one who'd set these houses on fire? Why would he even do that?

Colby didn't know.

But he needed to talk to Dillon.

Now.

THE SUN WAS BEGINNING to set as Emmy and Jeremy walked back to the inn.

She wanted to feel relaxed and like she was enjoying this evening. But there was just too much on her mind right now.

As they walked, the hair on Emmy's neck rose and she glanced behind her.

Were the earlier events of today playing on her mind? Maybe.

But another part of her felt like somebody was following them.

Her throat tightened at the thought.

Maybe walking to The Screen Porch Café this evening hadn't been the best idea. But now that the rain had faded, it had seemed perfect at the time.

Now, tension threaded through her.

"Everything okay?" Jeremy glanced over at her.

Emmy looked behind her again. "I just have this weird feeling right now."

Jeremy followed her gaze before jerking his eyes back to meet hers. "What kind of weird feeling?"

She rubbed her arms, wishing she could ward away her chill. But she couldn't. The freeze came from inside her.

"I know it's going to sound crazy, but I almost feel like someone's watching us right now," Emmy murmured.

Jeremy let out a nervous laugh, but the sound quickly faded. "That does sound a little crazy. But people always say you should listen to your gut instinct."

"That is what they say, isn't it?" She glanced over her shoulder again.

The sun was already beginning to set and weird shadows cast all around them. If somebody was watching them right now, he was doing a good job concealing himself.

"For a peaceful island, there sure does seem to be a lot going on," Jeremy said.

"You can say that again." Emmy's mind went back to the fire alarm she had heard earlier. She hoped that everything was okay. She hoped that *Colby* was okay—and Levi, of course. But Colby was the one out there fighting fires.

She wanted to call her friend and check on him. But she didn't. She knew Levi would let her know if anything happened.

With everything going on here on the island, Emmy's anxiety level was higher than usual.

Finally, Emmy and Jeremy reached the inn and walked to the door.

She'd done it. She had actually gone on her first date in years. Emmy would like to say that it felt good.

But that wouldn't entirely be the truth.

Even though Jeremy had been good company, he wasn't Colby. Still, that didn't mean Emmy thought she and Colby should continue exploring a possible romance between them.

There was too much on her mind right now, too many confusing thoughts and hard choices.

As they stood in front of the door, Emmy looked up at Jeremy, ready to thank him for the nice dinner.

Before she could, his lips covered hers.

Her entire body tensed. What was happening?

CHAPTER THIRTY-EIGHT

COLBY PAUSED HALFWAY between the station and the inn.

He desperately wanted to talk to Emmy right now, to tell her about what his father had done. Levi had picked Colby's dad up, and he'd admitted to the arsons.

Colby still couldn't believe it.

But Emmy could always help him to make sense of things.

He also wanted to talk about what he'd said to her earlier.

But halfway there, Colby spotted Emmy on the porch with Jeremy. The man leaned toward her and . . . kissed Emmy. What?

Colby held his breath as he stepped into the

shadows. He halfway hoped that Emmy might slap the man.

Instead, the two of them quietly spoke to each other. Colby couldn't make out what they said—not that it was his business.

Had Emmy already decided she liked Jeremy? If so, why hadn't she told him?

Colby's breathing turned heavier.

Had Emmy really liked Jeremy this whole time? Colby hoped he was simply reading too much into things. But it seemed clear he wasn't.

Before Emmy spotted him, Colby headed back to the station.

That job offer up in Virginia was looking more and more tempting all the time.

EMMY QUICKLY STEPPED AWAY from Jeremy, a queasy feeling in her stomach. She had *not* been expecting the man to kiss her—not by any stretch of the imagination.

She licked her lips before starting. "Jeremy..."

He frowned. "Did I misread things?"

Emmy drew in a breath, praying she'd have the right words. "I like to take things slow and..."

"And you're not sure there's anything here to take slowly?"

Emmy nodded apologetically. "Dinner was nice but . . ."

"I'm sorry." He shoved his hands into his pockets. "I misread the situation."

"It's okay." She rubbed her lips, wishing she could remove the feel of Jeremy's kiss. Wishing she could re-do this evening, for that matter.

Somehow, Jeremy's kiss seemed to erase her kiss with Colby earlier—and that wasn't what she wanted.

Jeremy pointed his thumb behind him. "I think I'll get back inside. It really was nice to have dinner with you."

"It was nice. Thank you."

As soon as he was gone, Emmy lowered herself onto the swing on her front porch.

She needed some time to sort through her thoughts.

So many things drifted through her mind that her head started to pound.

It was almost a relief when she saw Levi walking her way thirty minutes later. He sat beside her on the swing and stretched out his legs. Emmy could tell he knew something was going on. Had Colby talked to him?

"How are you?" he started.

"I've been better. You?"

He shrugged. "I've been better. I was hoping I might get a copy of those gravesites from you."

"Of course. I'll grab them. They're just inside."

"They can wait another moment," Levi said. "Have you talked to Colby?"

Her breath caught. What did she even say?

"We found the arsonist," Levi finally said.

She released her breath. Levi wasn't talking about Colby's feelings for Emmy. It was something else completely different. "What? I hadn't heard yet."

Levi frowned. "It was Colby's dad."

CHAPTER THIRTY-NINE

"COLBY IS PRETTY UPSET," Levi continued. "I thought he might have come over here to tell you."

Emmy shook her head, still trying to process everything. "No, things are a little awkward between us now."

Levi studied her a moment. "Colby told you he likes you?"

She nodded.

"And what did you tell him in response?"

Emmy shrugged. "Nothing. I was trying to figure out what to say when Jeremy stepped outside. I'd told him earlier that I'd go to dinner with him."

"Ouch." Levi flinched. "You like this Jeremy guy?"

Emmy didn't even have to think about her response. "No, I don't. But I told him we could have dinner together because I thought that might be a good step for me. I haven't dated in so long. I'm so used to saying no. But I wondered if . . . I wondered if I should start saying yes more."

"Was it a good first step for you?"

She frowned. "I guess the truth is . . . I'm still thinking about Colby."

"I'm sorry, Em. It sounds like you have some choices to make."

"I definitely do." She let out a long sigh before standing. "I'll get that map for you."

As Levi nodded, Emmy slipped inside the inn. Thankfully, she didn't pass Jeremy. She didn't want to talk to him anymore right now.

Instead, she slipped into her room and went to her desk, where she'd left the map earlier.

She pulled the drawer open and blinked.

The space was empty.

Where had her map gone?

Alarm raced through her.

Had someone been inside Emmy's house again?

COLBY LOOKED up as he heard somebody knock on the door to his office.

His heart raced when he saw Emmy standing there. "Can I come in?"

Even though his throat was tight, he managed to choke out, "Of course."

She stepped inside and closed the door behind her. After a moment of hesitation, she lowered herself in the seat across from him. "I heard about the fire. About your dad. I'm sorry."

"I shouldn't be surprised. He has a knack for trouble. He always has."

Emmy frowned. "Have you talked to him?"

"Levi's had a turn interrogating him, and now Grant is in with him. I'm not sure if there's anything productive that I can say right now."

"Did he say why?" Emmy studied his face as she waited for his response.

Colby shook his head, wishing there was more he could tell her. "I don't know. And I don't care. I've been enabling him for a long time now. Maybe some jail time is just what he needs to learn his lesson."

"I'm sorry, Colby."

He shrugged, trying to keep his emotions at bay. "It is what it is."

Emmy shifted. "Listen, Colby, I feel like we should talk about what happened earlier."

His dull gaze met hers. "It looks like your mind is already made up."

She froze, as if realizing she had been caught. "Colby, you and I have been friends for a long time."

"Listen, spare me the speech about how I'm a nice guy but . . . at least give me that much respect." He didn't think he could sit through one of those talks with Emmy.

"I didn't indicate that's what I was going to say."

"But I can hear it in your tone. That's what's coming."

She tilted her head, that sad look still present in her gaze. "Colby, you know how I am about relationships."

"But you were willing to give that Jeremy guy a chance?" Maybe he shouldn't have asked the question, but how could he not?

She opened her mouth, as if she wanted to explain but didn't know exactly how. "I'm . . . I have a lot to think about. I just need some time. So much is happening, and it's happening so fast."

Colby knew what that meant. Emmy was trying to think of a way to let him down easy.

That was Emmy.

She was always kind and thinking about other people's problems.

As she sat there staring at him with something that almost looked like pity in her gaze, Colby turned to his computer. "I'd love to talk more, but I have to help write a report."

Pain flashed in Emmy's eyes. Colby had probably never dismissed her before in their entire twenty years of knowing each other. But nothing had ever happened between them like it had today.

Emmy nodded, stood and stepped back. "I understand."

"One more thing you should know," Colby said.

Emmy paused. "What's that?"

"I'm going to head to Virginia tomorrow to meet with my friend about that job offer," he said. "I don't know what will come of it, but I figured I should at least ask some questions."

Her eyes widened a moment before she finally nodded, seeming to snap out of her surprised state. "Is that right? Wow. That's . . . that's great, Colby."

He shrugged. Colby had just made the decision, but it felt right. He needed some space from this town. From Emmy.

"I just wanted to let you know," he told her.

She nodded again. "You'll have to let me know how it goes."

With one last glance at him, Emmy slipped out the door.

As soon as she left, his mind reeled.

He may have just messed up things with his best friend. His dad was in jail. And from here on out, everybody was going to be looking at him like he was the son of an arsonist.

Maybe this *was* the perfect time for a new start.

CHAPTER FORTY

EMMY FELT beside herself the next morning.

Colby hadn't stopped by after work last night. He hadn't stopped by for breakfast in the morning. She hadn't heard from him all day.

Emmy understood he needed some space, but not having him in her life left Emmy with a void she didn't know was possible.

She'd started to pick up the phone and call Colby several times but had then changed her mind. Maybe this break would be good for them. Maybe some time apart would help both of them sort out their thoughts.

But Emmy's heart sagged with sadness. Sometimes she wished she could turn back time and forget everything that happened yesterday. That things could just go back to being the way they had been before.

But then she'd never know what it was like to feel Colby's lips against hers. She would never know the heart-pounding excitement of being close to him.

She had definitely felt something between them. The question was, was Emmy ready to pursue what a relationship between them might look like?

Sometimes she thought yes, but it was immediately followed by a fearful no.

Meanwhile, Jeremy had been upstairs in his room working today.

Levi's theory was that someone had snuck into Emmy's house while she and Jeremy were eating in order to steal that map with the various graves on it.

Levi's guys had been patrolling by the gravesites all day, but so far no one had shown up.

Finally, at about five o'clock that evening, Jeremy said he was going to go out for a walk.

Emmy waved to him as he left out the front door. She was halfway tempted just to stay in her room for the rest of the night moping about Colby not talking to her.

But she thought it would be a better idea to wash

the sheets in Jeremy's room. Emmy had an extra set she could put on in the meantime.

She slogged up the steps to do so.

As she took the blanket off and then stripped the bed, something fell on the floor.

Emmy leaned down to pick the object up and saw that it was a driver's license.

She frowned at the image there.

It was Jeremy's picture.

But not his name.

What sense did this make?

Emmy wasn't sure, but maybe she should tell Levi.

She got her phone, about to take a picture. That's when she sensed a shadowy presence in the doorway.

She froze a moment before slowly turning around.

Then she realized that she'd been caught red-handed.

"ARE you sure you want to do this?" Dillon asked as he sat behind his desk at the station.

Colby nodded, maintaining his stance in front of

Dillon. "I'm sure. I don't know that it will be forever, but I know I need to get away for now."

"Well, no one can blame you after everything that's happened with your father. But we're going to miss you around here."

Colby had decided last night that he was going to take a few days off work to visit his friend up in Norfolk, Virginia. He wanted to hear more about what this job would really be about.

The timing had been just right, almost like God had opened the door at the perfect time.

He wasn't saying he'd stay away from Cape Corral forever. But he would be staying away for now. It would be better this way.

"I feel better knowing that you have a lot of volunteer firefighters here to pick up the slack in my absence," Colby said.

Dillon's hands went to his hips. "Colby, you've come a long way since we first started working together. You're a great firefighter, and I've often wondered if you could take over as fire chief one day. I know I've been hard on you at times. It's only because I see potential inside you."

Colby's heart lurched into his throat. "That means a lot, Chief. Thank you."

The two exchanged a hearty handshake.

"And, if you could, keep an eye on Emmy," Colby said.

"You sure you don't want to do that?" Dillon raised his brow.

Colby swallowed hard. "I do. I really do. But I can't right now."

"I understand."

With one more glance back at the station, Colby grabbed his bag and stepped outside. He'd come back later and tell everyone else goodbye. Right now, he just needed to get out of here. The sooner, the better.

As soon as his feet hit the sand, he glanced at Emmy's inn.

His heart pounded in his ears as he pictured Emmy inside. What was she doing?

Part of him wanted to go over and tell Emmy goodbye. But another part of him knew that as soon as Emmy looked into his eyes, that there would be no way Colby could leave.

What he really needed right now was to go somewhere to clear his head. That meant getting away from this island and getting away from the sweet woman who'd broken his heart.

He'd call her later, he vowed.

Right now, Colby climbed into his truck and took

off toward a dock on the other side of the island. His friend was going to meet him there and take Colby via boat to the other side of the water, where he would borrow Dillon's truck for a little while.

Colby was going to go visit his friend and figure out if that job was the one for him or not.

At least now the arsonist was in jail. No more graves had been dug up. And maybe Colby could work on getting over everything that had happened.

CHAPTER FORTY-ONE

EMMY TOOK a step back as she felt a tremble rake through her.

Suddenly, everything made sense. Maybe not everything. But enough.

Enough that Emmy knew she was in trouble.

"Jeremy." Her voice sounded scratchy, though she willed it to be normal. "I was just . . . changing your sheets."

His gaze looked dark and stormy. "You shouldn't have come in here."

Emmy tried to play it cool, even though she knew she had been caught. Running wasn't an option right now—Jeremy blocked the door.

"I try to change the sheets at least once a week for my long-term guests."

Jeremy stepped closer, his gaze darkening. "You and I both know that's not what this is about."

Emmy reached for her neck. Her mouth went dry with every new word that was spoken. This wasn't a bad dream or a misunderstanding. The danger emanating from Jeremy was all too real.

"What do you mean?" she finally asked, trying to buy some time until she could come up with an escape plan.

Emmy wished she had something on her. A gun. Mace. Her cell phone.

Instead, she felt trapped with nowhere to go and nothing to defend herself with.

Jeremy's voice dipped low until the menace there was unmistakable. "You weren't supposed to see that license."

Emmy decided to drop her act. Pretending to be clueless was only drawing this out. "Why are you using the identity of a dead man?"

"It's a long story. But now that this is all out in the open, I am going to need your help figuring out a few things. Whoever thought it would be so fortuitous when you hit me in that truck."

"What are you actually doing here on the island, Jeremy? Or should I call you Luther?"

He tugged at his shirt, almost as if he was getting nervous. "Luther works."

"You're the one who broke into the station and smashed the computers, aren't you? You overheard that Levi was going to get information on that dead man's real identity."

He shrugged. "I couldn't risk being discovered."

"Did you push me into that grave?"

He hesitated a moment. "It's not important right now. We don't have time to play these games. I haven't been on this island that long, but I've been here long enough to know that everybody here knows everyone else's business. You seem to have at least six adopted older brothers who are watching out for your every move. No doubt one of them is going to be stopping by at any time now. That means we need to move."

Another shot of fear made her bones tremble. "Where are we going?"

"You'll see. But for now, let's get out of here."

"I don't think that's a good idea." Emmy knew she shouldn't go anywhere with the man. Her odds were better if she stayed here. But how could she convince him of that?

Jeremy—or Luther, as the license read—reached behind him and pulled out something.

A gun.

"I have this, and I'm not afraid to use it. I'm not afraid to use it on *you*, but I think it would be entirely more effective if I threaten to use this on somebody that you care about. Are we clear?" His gaze darkened even more.

All at once, visions of all the people Emmy cared about flashed through her mind. She'd never forgive herself if somebody got hurt because of her. She simply couldn't let that happen.

"We're clear." Her voice wavered as she said the words.

"Good. Now, we're going to walk to your truck as if we're just two people spending time together. If anybody asks, you're going to give me a tour of the island. I'm going to repeat this one more time. Do you understand?"

Emmy stared at the gun as she nodded. "I understand."

She had no doubt that this man would use that gun on her if he felt threatened enough.

COLBY WAS CRUISING across the water in his friend's Bayliner when his phone rang. He glanced at the screen and saw it was Levi.

For a moment, he contemplated not answering.

But Levi knew Colby was leaving. So, if he was calling, he probably had a good reason for it.

"Hey, man," Colby answered. "What's up?"

"Have you seen Emmy?" Levi asked. "She's not with you by chance, is she?"

Concern instantly gripped him. "Emmy? No, she's not with me. Why?"

"I've been trying to call her for the past hour or so, but she hasn't been answering her phone. I already checked the inn, and she's not there either. The non-responsiveness isn't like her."

Colby's concern intensified. "You're right. That's not like her. Maybe she went somewhere, and she's out of range."

"Maybe. But Emmy knows to tell me first."

Colby couldn't argue with that. Levi and Emmy looked out for each other. That's the way it had always been.

"I'll head back and help you find her," Colby said.

"You don't have to do that. I will keep looking. I just thought I should check with you first."

Colby clamped down his jaw as he considered his options. Should he turn around? Or did he just need to walk away and not look back?

He wasn't sure.

Finally, Colby told Levi, "I hope you find her."

"Me too. I'm sure this is nothing."

But Colby knew that if Levi had called him, that this wasn't nothing.

Colby prayed Emmy was okay.

But a bad feeling brewed in his gut.

CHAPTER FORTY-TWO

"WHERE ARE WE GOING?" Emmy asked Jeremy—or Luther. She was having trouble thinking of the man as anyone other than Jeremy.

They bumped down the road in Emmy's truck. Luther was driving, but he had his gun in his lap and it was aimed at her.

She knew if she made any wrong moves, pain would follow.

"I need you to show me those graves," he said.

The graves . . . they were what this boiled down to. But why?

"I can't show you the other graves," Emmy said. "The map I had of them was stolen."

He reached into his pocket and tossed something into her lap. "Here it is."

She sucked in a quick breath. "You're the one who stole this?"

He shrugged, as if unfazed by his actions. "It worked out well. You were on that porch for a long time—just long enough for me to go in and grab it."

"I don't understand. Why do you need this map? Why are these graves so important?"

"It's a long story."

"It seems like we have plenty of time."

"We have less time than you think. If I don't find what I'm looking for, then we're both going to be dead."

Her mind swam for a minute. Both of them would be dead? What did that even mean?

"I've been to all of these graves, and I didn't see anything at any of them that would make it appear that they are anything special," Emmy finally said.

"But you mentioned that there was one other graveyard you'd discovered after you made this map."

"Yes, but . . ."

His hard gaze locked onto hers. "That's where I need to go. You need to tell me how to get there."

Emmy chomped down for a moment before nodding. She really had no other options at this point.

As they bumped down the sandy road, a couple of people from town spotted them and waved.

"Act normal," Luther said through gritted teeth. "People in town did see us on a date yesterday, so this shouldn't seem weird."

Emmy did what he said, trying to look like this was just an ordinary outing. But questions continued to race through her mind. "Did you purposefully run out in front of my truck, just so you could get to me?"

He shrugged. "It was fortuitous, I suppose. I was headed to the inn to see if I could stay there. But the rest of the story is true. I accidentally stumbled in front of your truck."

"So if you're not really Jeremy, then who was the real Jeremy Riesling?"

"I don't know why you're asking so many questions," Luther muttered. "None of this matters."

"It obviously does matter if you're going to all this trouble." The more Emmy knew, the more ammunition she would have to talk her way out of this.

His gaze darkened. "If you must know, Jeremy was my coworker. I followed him here to Cape Corral."

"Why would you do that? Did you kill him?" A sickly feeling roiled in her gut.

"No, I didn't kill him. But the person who's going to kill both you and I, did. That should light a fire under you."

Her chest tightened as she thought about Luther's words. "So you followed your coworker here and stole his identity. That still doesn't make any sense to me. And why was my address in that man's pocket?"

"He wanted to get this map from you. He was doing research and saw the article about your project. If he couldn't find the grave on his own, visiting you was next on his list."

Emmy shuddered.

Luther muttered something under his breath before saying, "Where do I need to turn?"

Emmy pointed up ahead. "There. We'll have to walk after you park."

"Jeremy had a big mouth," Luther finally explained. "I overheard him talking about how he found some old documents his ancestors left him. One of them was about a man who died in 1889. He said he was buried with his treasure. Gold—gold he'd found after a shipwreck."

Emmy processed that news, the growing feeling

of disgust growing in her stomach. "So all of this is about money?"

"Money is pretty important, especially when you have someone chasing after you to get what you owe."

"So you're in debt," she muttered, things making even more sense. "How did you get to be in this debt?" She studied his face for a minute. "I don't think it's drugs. It's gambling, isn't it?"

His gaze narrowed even more. "You're smarter than I thought you were. If I don't find this money within the next twenty-four hours, it's all over. That's really all you need to know."

COLBY SPRINTED INSIDE THE STATION. There was no way he could go to Virginia—not if there was a possibility that Emmy was in trouble.

He should have known better than to leave in the first place.

As soon as he saw Grant at his desk, he sensed the tension in the air.

He knew what that meant.

No one had seen Emmy still.

"What's going on?" Colby stared at Grant. "Where is everyone?"

"Emmy was seen riding down the road with her boarder. Everyone's out looking for them now—except me. I'm monitoring the station until we know more."

"I take it that's not good news." Colby sensed there was more to this story.

Grant frowned. "The real Jeremy Riesling isn't the man who was staying with Emmy. Jeremy Riesling is the man who died."

Concern ricocheted through Colby, and he leaned against the doorframe to keep his balance. "What?"

"Apparently, this man staying with Emmy stole the dead man's identity. Everything he's told us has been a lie."

"Do we have any idea why?" What sense did that make?

"We still don't know this guy's real name, so, no, we don't know yet. But if someone's willing to go to all that trouble, then something bad is at the center of it."

"Do we think this guy killed the real Jeremy Riesling?" The thought caused a sickly feeling to form in Colby's gut.

"Based on that man's time of death and the time that Emmy hit him, it seems doubtful. But we're not ruling anything out right now. He had the real Jeremy Riesling's wallet and phone on him. When Levi went over to the inn and checked out the man's room, they were in a drawer there."

"I can't believe that . . . we saw the man's driver's license. It looked real."

"He must have paid someone to create it for him before he came here."

Colby shook his head. "So, the house where the fake Jeremy went to get his things . . . wasn't that rented in his name?"

Grant nodded. "In the real Jeremy's name. This other guy must have known he was staying there. Did you ever notice how his clothes didn't really fit him? Maybe that's because they weren't his real clothes."

Just then, Grant's phone rang. He talked to the person on the other end of the line before ending the call and turning to Colby.

"More bad news," he started. "We got a hit on this guy's identity. He's someone named Luther Sterling. Apparently, he roughed up Jeremy Riesling's roommate in order to find out where he was going. He heard something about some money that had been buried here on the island, and he wanted to get his hands on it."

"Why?"

"He has some gambling debts. He probably had to take an alternate identity because the police up in New Hampshire have a warrant out for his arrest."

More pieces began to click in place. But Colby didn't like the picture it formed.

Just then, someone else stepped into the station. Colby turned and saw Gilbert Davies standing near the entrance. The man's eyebrows scrunched as if he sensed the tension also.

"I feel like this is a bad time," he started, taking a step back. "I just had some questions about the survey I'm doing in the area for the environmental study."

Grant rose from his desk and strode toward him. "If you wouldn't mind, could we do this tomorrow instead?"

Gilbert pushed up his glasses and glanced around again, not bothering to hide his curiosity. "Of course. I hope that everything is okay."

"We just have some personal matters we're attending to right now."

"Of course." Gilbert glanced around one more time. "I'll come back tomorrow. In the meantime, and if it's any consolation, I don't think it's going to be a problem to get this environmental measure passed. But we'll talk more about that tomorrow."

"That sounds great." Grant tilted his head at the man. "Tomorrow."

Tomorrow seemed like a really long time away, Colby noted. Because right now, all he could think about was finding Emmy.

If they didn't find Emmy today, then tomorrow was going to look a lot bleaker. Not just for Colby . . . but for everyone here on the island.

CHAPTER FORTY-THREE

HE WAS SO close to getting what he wanted.

He could feel it.

He was on the cusp of seeing his plan completed.

Just a few more steps, and he'd be done.

A smile curled his lips.

This had been surprisingly easy.

But he couldn't get cocky.

There was still more work to be done.

More lives to end.

But he had a plan for that also.

He'd even put together a kit as part of an emergency strategy for his getaway. Everything he needed was tucked away, ready to be used.

And the islanders would be none the wiser about any of it.

His smile widened.

It was time to get busy.

CHAPTER FORTY-FOUR

"HOW DO you know it's at this grave and not one of the others?" Emmy asked as she and Luther trekked through the thick woods to find the grave he was looking for.

"I've checked the other graves," he muttered.

"But I saw them earlier. They weren't disturbed."

"I checked them earlier in the week before the floodwaters came. But then I discovered where the more recent ones were. I didn't have time to fill them in."

"Do you really think finding this gold is going to solve all your problems?" Dry grass cracked at her feet and barren, early winter branches scratched at anything in their way.

"I know it will. Why do you have to keep asking

all these questions? You seem like a nice enough lady. In fact, there's part of me that really does like you. I'm sorry that you had to get involved with this. I didn't have any other choice."

Emmy swallowed hard, doubting his words.

"How much farther?" he asked.

Emmy tried to recall what she'd learned about those recently uncovered cemeteries. "I'm totally going off my memory, but maybe another mile or so."

He muttered something underneath his breath again. "We're never going to get there in time."

"What's going to happen if you do find this gold? You think you're just going to carry it off this island and leave?"

"Something like that." His nostrils flared.

"Gold is heavy."

"I'm not stupid. I know that."

"I just thought I would point that out, just in case," Emmy said.

"Thank you for your input."

They continued to push through the brush. As the sun continued to sink, the air became colder. Emmy also knew that the darker it was outside, the harder it would be for anyone to find them.

Was anyone even looking?

She knew that her brother would probably come and check on her. It wouldn't be long before he realized something was wrong, if he didn't already.

And what about Colby? Did he know Emmy was missing? Did he care?

The thought of him made sadness fill her chest.

Colby certainly hadn't taken the news well that Emmy needed to think things over before taking the plunge into a relationship.

But there was nothing else that she could do about that. Not now, at least.

Finally, she pointed to something in the distance. "It's right over there."

She indicated some tombstones that rose above the brush.

Luther smiled and handed her a shovel. "Perfect. Now you start digging. One wrong move, and I'll shoot."

***

"COLBY." Levi strode down the hall toward him. "Emmy's disappearance has to tie in with those gravesites that have been dug up. Do you remember anything about that map Emmy showed you?"

Colby shrugged, his shoulders tight. "I wish I did,

but Emmy was the one holding it and telling me where to go. I was just along for the ride."

Levi's lips flickered down in a frown. "We've had our men keeping an eye on several of those graves, but there hasn't been any action there."

"Emmy did say something about a graveyard she discovered after she wrote this paper in high school."

Levi's gaze sparked with interest. "Did she happen to mention that in front of Jeremy?"

"As a matter of fact, I think that he was in the other room."

"If he overheard that, and he *is* behind some of these grave robberies, then maybe that's where they're headed right now."

Colby shook his head, beating himself up for not asking more questions. "I wish I could remember where Emmy said that other graveyard was, but I don't even think she told me a specific location. She just mentioned she'd found it."

"We need to find someone here on this island who might know something about it. We don't have time to do a grid search of everything. Not with Emmy gone missing like she is."

"I can talk to some of the old-timers here and see if they remember anything," Colby said.

"Why don't you do that?" Levi said. "I'll do the same. Maybe between the two of us we'll be able to figure something out."

Colby nodded, but his heart felt heavy. What he really wanted was to be out there searching for Emmy.

But Levi was right. They would be wasting entirely too much time if they wandered around this island aimlessly searching.

Colby knew who he wanted to start with.

His father.

His dad knew this island better than anybody else. And as much as Colby dreaded talking to his dad. He would do it.

Only if it meant finding Emmy.

EMMY PAUSED for long enough to wipe the sweat from her brow. Even though it was chilly outside, digging this old grave up was hard work.

Especially when Luther had his gun aimed on her the whole time.

His eyes had a wild look to them, and Emmy had no doubt the man would pull the trigger if it came down to it. At this point, she could be nothing more than a casualty.

What else did he have to lose? If he didn't get this gold, he was a dead man anyway.

Finally, the shovel hit something.

Luther perked up as he stepped closer. "Finish clearing the grave and then open the casket."

Dread filled Emmy's stomach. The last thing she

wanted to do was to open a grave that was more than a hundred years old. But what other choice did she have?

Her arms ached as she continued to dig. Finally, an old casket appeared beneath her feet. She paused from digging to look at Luther, briefly wondering if she could swing the shovel and knock the gun out of his hand.

But she was too deep in this hole. It wouldn't do her any good.

Instead, she placed the shovel on the ground beside her and waited for further instructions.

"Open it," Luther ordered.

"How? With my bare hands?"

He handed her something he'd grabbed from the truck. A crowbar. Her crowbar, one she kept in the back in case of emergencies.

"No, with this."

"Aren't you prepared?" she muttered.

"What can I say? I try."

Emmy shoved the crowbar beneath the top of the coffin. A few moves later, the wood splintered.

Her heart pounded into her chest as she waited to see what she might find.

Was this the treasure Luther had been so desperate to locate?

She pried more of the top off before she was finally able to pull it back. As she did, an old skeleton stared back at her.

Emmy gasped as bile rose in her throat.

But once she looked at the skeleton, she noticed that it was just that—a skeleton and nothing else.

"Move the skeleton," Luther ordered.

"What?" Emmy asked. "You want me to touch him?"

"Did I stutter?"

She hesitated as she looked at the bones in front of her.

Then she looked back at Luther with his gun.

She knew she had no choice but to do as he said.

***

"SON." His dad stared across the interrogation table at Colby, his eyes haggard and bloodshot. "I wasn't expecting to see you."

He looked awful with his red eyes, pale skin, and wild frizzy hair.

"I'm only here because I'm desperate," Colby said.

"What's going on?"

"Emmy is missing, and we need to find her. We

think she went out looking for a gravesite on the island—maybe somewhere secluded that most people don't know about. You know this island well. You spend most of your days fishing or wandering aimlessly. Have you seen any gravesites?"

His dad ran his hand through his thinning hair. "I've seen a lot of gravesites."

"I'm talking about ones that most people don't know about."

His dad didn't say anything for a moment. Colby felt the frustration rising in him, and he tried to hold it at bay. But they didn't have a lot of time here.

Why couldn't his dad get his act together? Why couldn't he think about someone other than himself for once in his life?

Finally, his dad's eyes met Colby's. "I did it for you, you know."

Colby tensed. What did that mean? "What are you talking about?"

"Those houses that burned. I wanted to make a statement. I wanted to do something bold."

"But you can't burn people's houses down." Had his dad lost his mind?

"Everybody in town was trying to be so nice in order to change the Fergusons' minds, and it wasn't working. I decided to try some more drastic measures. You know what I used for an ignitor, don't you?"

"What's that?"

"My alcohol." His dad smiled. "It was perfect. I got rid of the liquor and sent a message to the Fergusons."

"You shouldn't have set their houses on fire, Dad." Colby shook his head, fighting frustration. "You should know better than to do that."

"Don't lecture me, son. I know I've made a lot of mistakes. I was trying to make things right."

"You make things right by trying to be a good person."

"I know I failed you when you were a child, son. I'm sorry for that."

Colby shook his head. "Are you? Because if you were sorry, you would have changed. You would have given up alcohol. You would have been there for me when I needed you."

"And I regret that every day."

Colby found that hard to believe. "But you're still drinking."

"I haven't had a sip in five weeks, as a matter of fact."

Colby wanted to believe his dad was telling the truth. But life experience told him not to. "Emmy's life may depend on you remembering where those gravesites are."

His dad moaned and lowered his head.

He still didn't have an answer for Colby, did he? Colby should have known better.

Finally, Colby stood. He couldn't waste any more time here. He'd already wasted enough. "I hope you know you're probably going to be spending quite a bit of time in jail, Dad. Maybe it will be good for you."

"I have no doubt that I deserve it." His dad raised his head, his blue eyes full of angst.

As Colby stepped toward the door, his dad spoke again.

"There was another graveyard about three hundred yards from the Jezebel Tree. Go north. There are about eight tombstones there. Maybe that's what you're looking for."

CHAPTER FORTY-SIX

EMMY'S EYES widened when she saw what was beneath the body. She'd used the crowbar to move the skeletal remains so she wouldn't have to touch the bones.

A tattered cloth was there with something protruding beneath it.

Carefully, she moved the crowbar again to reveal the contents.

Old eelgrass stared back.

Eelgrass? Had it really been preserved all these years?

Just beneath it, something glimmered.

Emmy sucked in a breath.

Sure enough, eight gold bars were there.

She looked up at Luther and saw his eyes widen.

He'd found what he wanted.

The gold was actually here.

"I knew it!" A smile spread across his face. "I knew that letter was true."

As much as Emmy would like to delight in this moment with him, she had other concerns. "What now?"

"Hand them up to me." Luther reached down, ready to take one.

Emmy went to pick one up. As she did, she saw Luther put his gun down.

Was this her chance to make a move?

Even if Emmy managed to hit Luther or knock him out, how would she get out of this hole?

Even more so, should she take the chance?

The questions pummeled her.

There were no easy answers here.

She gripped one of the gold bars and handed it up to Luther. He lifted it toward his face and a huge grin stretched across his lips.

"You have no idea how much this is going to change my life."

Disgust roiled in her stomach. How could this man possibly think that somebody else's life wasn't as important as this gold?

"Hand me the next one," he ordered.

Emmy leaned down and grabbed the gold. As Luther moved to take it from her, she made a split-second decision and grabbed his wrist.

Before he realized what was happening, she pulled him into the grave with her. Before he could rise to his feet, she snatched up the crowbar and held it over her shoulder.

If she didn't try to take control of this situation, Luther was going to shoot her.

She had no doubt about that.

***

"THAT'S EMMY'S TRUCK." Colby pointed to the vehicle in the distance.

"They must have gone in the woods," Levi said. "Maybe this guy thought Emmy could lead him to the other gravesites."

Levi pulled over behind the truck. Two other vehicles pulled in behind them.

Levi had utilized the rest of the team, as well as several volunteers. Colby had told him what his father said about the grave.

They climbed out and met with the rest of the guys. Even though his dad had given him a basic location, searching these woods was a big job. The trees were thick and the landscape rolling.

Colby looked out over the woods, trying not to feel overwhelmed. "It's going to take a while to search everything."

"We better get busy," Levi said. "Let's split up, but we need to stay in touch with each other. If we find this guy, we don't need to confront him alone. Does everybody understand?"

The team around them nodded.

"Then let's get going," Levi said.

Colby entered the woods and headed south, trying to find the area his dad had told him about.

Maybe his father would finally redeem himself. Not that this would make up for all the years of emotional abuse his dad had given him. But maybe it would be a starting point, at least.

As Colby trudged through the woods, he tried to remain quiet. He wanted to hear it if anybody was out here.

He still had at least a mile to go until he reached the Jezebel Tree and then another three hundred or so feet north to walk beyond that. Now that the darkness was falling, everything seemed more complicated.

His thoughts bounced all over the place.

First to Emmy.

If Colby had to do it over again, he'd still tell her how he felt about her. Emmy was the best thing to ever happen to him. She was worth the risk.

He prayed again that she was okay.

He crossed a murky ditch, walking over a fallen log to do so. As he did, he glanced down and saw a snake in the water below.

These woods weren't a safe place for anyone to be. Even though Emmy could handle herself. He still hated the thought of her being out here.

And what about Jeremy—the fake one? How could he have pulled the wool over their eyes?

How could Colby's father have set those fires?

There was so much going wrong in his life right now.

All he knew was that he had to find Emmy before anything would be right again.

CHAPTER FORTY-SEVEN

"WHAT DO you think you're doing?" Luther seethed as he pulled himself to his feet. Dirt stuck to his skin, and his eyes were narrowed with anger.

Emmy held the crowbar, trying to hide her nerves. She knew there was no use. It was evident in the way her hands trembled as well as her voice.

"I'm not going to let you kill me and leave me here," she grumbled.

"You really think you're going to be able to hit me with that?" His eyes lit, almost as if he were amused. "I don't know you, but I know that you're not the type."

"Don't test me." Emmy gripped the crowbar tighter.

Could she swing it? She wanted to say yes. But she wasn't sure of the real answer.

"Why don't we talk this through?" Luther's voice sank, as if he were employing a different side of his personality.

The man was a manipulator, and Emmy wasn't going to fall for it again.

"There's nothing to talk through. After you have this gold, you have no reason to keep me alive." Emmy had already thought about it.

This grave wasn't going to be *her* grave.

"I'm a gambler, not a killer," Luther insisted. "I just needed your help."

"I find that doubtful," Emmy said through gritted teeth.

This man had been nothing more than an actor. His name wasn't real, his affable demeanor wasn't real, his kiss certainly wasn't real—not that Emmy wanted it to be.

Emmy knew they only had a couple of hours of daylight left. Once the sun started to sink, wild animals would come out. The temperature would drop. Finding anyone would become harder.

"Now you have me down here," Luther murmured. "What exactly are you planning on doing? Are we just going to stay down here and talk?

And if you kill me, how are you going to get out of this hole?"

His questions were valid, but Emmy couldn't let the doubt show in her eyes. "Maybe I'll just keep you occupied until someone finds us."

He let out a harsh chuckle. "Who do you think is going to find you? Does anyone even know you're out here?"

"I have friends. They'll come looking for me. I know them well enough to know that." She couldn't let this man get into her head.

Luther stared at her another moment, challenge in his gaze.

Suddenly, he lunged at her.

Emmy raised the crowbar higher, ready to swing.

But before she could, a gunshot rang through the air.

She froze, unsure where the sound came from.

The next instant, Luther sank to his knees. His wide eyes stared at her as the last touch of life left his body.

Then he collapsed, falling onto the skeleton in the coffin.

COLBY FROZE when he heard the gunfire.

His heart quickened as Emmy's image filled his mind.

What if someone had hurt her?

He grabbed his radio to talk to Levi. "Did you hear that?"

"It sounded like it came from about a half a mile south of us."

That's what Colby had thought too.

The exact area where Emmy could be.

He quickened his steps. What if that man had shot her?

Anger pushed through his veins.

If someone hurt Emmy . . . Colby wasn't sure what he would do. Part of him didn't want to find out what he'd do to that person if he got his hands on him.

Right now, all he cared about was finding Emmy.

He kept pushing through the woods. Faster and faster. Not much longer, and he should be at the area his father told him about.

As he got closer, he heard movement.

He froze.

But when he looked over, Levi stood across the woods.

The two of them nodded at each other before continuing to move forward.

Colby stopped ten feet later.

A mound of dirt was in front of him, along with the hole.

Colby held his breath as he peered inside. He dreaded what he might find there.

Please, not Emmy. Please!

His eyes widened when he saw the man who'd pretended to be Jeremy Riesling.

His body laid at the bottom of the grave. Blood stained his chest.

The man was clearly dead.

But there was no sign of Emmy.

Where had she gone?

CHAPTER FORTY-EIGHT

"WHO ARE YOU?" Emmy asked as the man gripped her arm, shoving her through the woods.

She'd never seen him before. He was probably in his forties. His build was slight but strong. His hair, light brown. His features almost delicate—deceivingly so.

Because this man was a cold-blooded killer.

He'd shot Luther and acted like he didn't even think anything about it.

"It's not important," the man growled. "We just need to get moving."

"What are you going to do with me?"

"You'll see. I'm going to create a distraction that will ensure people are so busy saving you that they don't even have time to see me getting away. I had a backup plan. I like to think of myself as always being prepared. Thankfully, you won't have to walk too far. In that sense, this could be much worse for you."

The man had insisted that Emmy give him the gold. He'd put it into a backpack. Then he had helped her out of the grave.

Now, they walked at a fast clip the opposite way through the woods. Emmy had nearly stumbled several times, but the man's grip had remained tight.

"You're the man Luther owed the money to," Emmy muttered.

"You are a bright girl."

"You're also the one who killed the real Jeremy, aren't you?"

"He caught me snooping around, and I had no choice," the man said. "It wasn't what I wanted to do, but, when push comes to shove, you must re-examine your priorities."

Luther may have been desperate for the money, but this man had no concept of right or wrong. If Emmy had thought she'd been in danger before, then she was definitely in danger now.

Instead of walking deeper into the woods, the man cut to the east where the woods ended.

What exactly was his plan?

"Not much further," he grumbled.

"You don't really think you'll get away with this, do you?" Emmy muttered.

"I'm going to do my best. I have a lot of money I need to spend. It would be a shame if anything got in the way of that."

"How can you even live with yourself?"

"I find ways. Believe me I do."

A few minutes later, they emerged from the woods. Emmy glanced around, but it was shadowy outside as daylight continued to fade. No doubt most of the men, if they were even in the area, were now trying to track down the source of the earlier gunfire.

Nobody was probably even looking this way yet—just as the man had hoped.

The man's grip remained strong on Emmy as he pulled her toward a house in the distance.

One of the Fergusons' places, Emmy realized.

It looked unoccupied right now.

A bad feeling brewed in her gut.

As he dragged her up the steps and into the house, she saw the can of gasoline sitting by the door.

This man hadn't heard that the arsonist had been caught, had he?

That was her best guess.

She knew exactly what was going to happen next.

Fear nearly consumed her at the thought.

"WHERE DID EMMY GO?" Colby glanced around, searching the woods for any sign of her.

"Maybe there's a second man involved here," Levi said. "If so, he must have taken her somewhere. If we didn't pass him going this way, that must mean he headed in the opposite direction."

Colby stepped that way. "I'll start searching."

Levi grabbed his arm before he could go any farther. "This guy is obviously unhinged. We have to be careful. I'm going to call in the state police so they can help us out right now."

"All I want to do is find Emmy."

"Me too." Levi's voice cracked. "Believe me, me too. We just need to keep a cool head right now. I'm going to let the other guys know what is going on."

Colby knelt on the ground. "There are footprints here."

"Can you track them?"

"I can do my best."

"Do that. I'm going to be right behind you."

Colby didn't wait any longer. He began following the tracks through the woods.

He only hoped that he found Emmy in time.

Because he didn't know what this guy was planning to do with her.

But he knew that it couldn't be good.

THE MAN JERKED Emmy's hands behind her with some rope he'd left inside the house. "I can't make it too easy for you to get away."

"You're not going to get away with this," Emmy muttered.

The man smiled. "Just you wait."

"People are going to know that I was tied up inside. They're going to look for you."

"Not necessarily. Not when the ropes burn off— along with the rest of you." The man flashed a smile.

Fear trembled through her. Death by fire?

Emmy wouldn't wish that on her worst enemy.

"You just happened to have all this stuff here?" Emmy asked.

"I thought I might have to use this on Luther, but

it's your lucky day." He flashed a grin, almost as if he enjoyed this. "I've been scoping out places all week. So many homes on this side of the island are unoccupied. That made this even more perfect—just the solution I needed."

"Why don't you just leave me here and run?" Emmy figured trying a new tactic couldn't hurt. What did she have to lose? "There's still time for you to get away."

"Don't try to bargain with me," the man growled. "I've already figured out what I want to do."

"But there are other ways."

He took something from his pocket and shoved it into her mouth. It was an old rag of some kind. "I'm tired of hearing you talk."

Emmy practically gagged on the foul cloth. But as much as she tried, she couldn't get it out of her mouth. It tasted like dirt and sweat.

The man knelt down and tied her feet to a chair as well. Then he shoved her back against a wall in the living room. Emmy's eyes widened as he took the can of gasoline and began to spread it around the room.

The distinct scent rose around her until she felt like she might throw up.

Emmy couldn't do that. She might choke on her own vomit.

She needed all the time she could to figure out how to get out of this.

If the man turned his back, she might be able to scoot in her chair across the room.

But as soon as he lit a match and this gasoline began to burn, this whole place was going to go up.

There was no way Emmy could move fast enough to get away.

Tears pressed her eyes.

What if there wasn't a way to get out of this?

What if this was the way it was all going to end?

COLBY FOLLOWED the tracks as they led from the woods.

As he emerged from the tree line, he glanced around, looking for a sign as to where Emmy might be.

A few houses were in front of him, nestled on the rolling sand dunes.

Where would they have gone from here? Had there been a truck waiting nearby that the man had driven away in?

Colby glanced at the ground but didn't see any recent tire prints.

Instead, his gaze went to the homes in the distance.

He sucked in a breath.

They were in Ferguson territory, he realized.

Many of these houses sat untouched right now in the cold weather. Could this man have taken Emmy into one of them?

Colby searched the ground again for prints, but the wind was just strong enough here that it pushed the sand over any potential tracks.

But Colby couldn't let that stop him.

He was going to try a few of the closest houses to see if anybody was there.

He pulled out his radio and gave Levi a quick update.

Then he started looking, knowing he had no time to waste.

CHAPTER FIFTY

EMMY DESPERATELY WANTED TO TALK. Wanted to argue her case.

But she couldn't.

She felt helpless as she watched the man spill more gasoline on the floor. He sloshed the liquid throughout the room until his can was empty.

Then he turned to her with a malicious grin on his face. "I'm sorry it has to end this way. I really am. You seem like a nice person."

Emmy shook her head, pleading with him with her gaze.

It was no use.

The man was unaffected. Cold. Hardened.

Her gaze darted around as she desperately tried to find a way out of this. But any angle she looked at it, help was too far away. Her binds hindered her too much.

Dear Lord . . . help me. Please!

"Well, it's been fun." The man reached into his pocket and pulled out a lighter. "But I'm afraid this is going to have to come to an end."

Emmy shook her head again, still desperate to get through to him. Her eyes widened as she tried to let this man know he didn't have to do this.

But he raised the lighter, determination in his gaze and satisfaction in his smile.

This was it. This was how it was all going to end.

If only she'd had the chance to tell the people she loved goodbye. Especially Colby . . .

Warm tears flooded her gaze at the thought.

Just then, the door burst open behind him.

Colby rushed into the house.

Colby.

He'd found her.

But Emmy's relief was short lived.

Because the man in front of her was about to ignite that lighter and end it all for her.

COLBY SMELLED the gas in the air.

The man in front of him was going to light this place up.

With Emmy inside.

Anger flared to life inside him.

Especially when he saw Emmy tied up in the chair with a gag in her mouth.

He gripped his gun, knowing backup was on the way.

But Colby couldn't wait. If Emmy was going to survive this, it was up to him.

"Put the gun down or I set her on fire," the man grumbled. "Don't test me."

Colby knew he couldn't pull this trigger anyway. There was too much gasoline in the air. He couldn't risk the chamber firing and causing a spark that sent this place up in the flames.

"Put it down!" the man yelled again.

"I will." Slowly, Colby set his Glock on the floor in front of him.

"Use your foot to push it toward me."

Colby did as he said. When he looked back up, his gaze went to the man's face and he sucked in a breath. "Gilbert?"

The man smirked. "Not really. I just heard some people in town talking, saying an environmentalist was coming. I decided to get creative. I figured I needed a good reason to be here in Cape Corral. It was even better that my supposed role gave me access to the police station and fire crew."

Colby glanced at Emmy. "Why bring her into this? She doesn't have anything to do with what's happening here."

"Unfortunately, she's collateral damage. I guess you will be also." Gilbert held up his lighter. "Unless you back out of this room, you're going to be toast too."

Colby blocked the doorway, his muscles bristling. "Is that right?"

The man's smile dimmed. "I've got all the power here. You need to realize that."

"If this place goes up in flames, you're going with it."

"I don't think so." Doubt flashed through the man's gaze though his voice remained smooth.

"I don't know how you plan on proving me wrong. As a firefighter, I'd say I have a really solid idea of how fire works."

The man snatched Colby's gun from the floor and pointed it at Colby. "Then maybe I should use this."

Colby's eyes widened when he realized how clueless this man was concerning the danger he was putting himself in. "Pull the trigger, and none of us will walk out of here. The bullet will ignite the gasoline vapors, and this whole place will light up."

The man's smile disappeared as he seemed to realize the truth of Colby's words.

They'd come to a proverbial impasse. If this man wanted to get away, he was going to have to pull the trigger. But if he pulled the trigger, he'd be putting his own life at risk also.

Colby waited for the man's next move.

He prayed for the best.

But, whatever happened, he wasn't leaving Emmy.

CHAPTER FIFTY-ONE

AN EQUAL MIX of relief and fear shot through Emmy when she saw Colby.

Relief because he could help.

Fear because he could get hurt.

How were they going to get out of this situation in one piece?

She had no idea.

The maniac with the lighter didn't seem interested in backing down.

Emmy knew Colby enough to know that he wouldn't either.

Please, Lord. Help us! Protect Colby. Show Your justice on this situation.

As the men talked, she leaned forward and tried

to catch the gag in her mouth between her knees. She couldn't quite reach . . .

She tried again.

Finally, on the third attempt, she managed to squeeze the cloth between her knees and jerk the rag from her mouth.

She swallowed hard and gulped in a deep breath of air.

She didn't have time to revel in the moment.

She needed to think.

She had to undo the ropes that bound her wrists and ankles. She needed something that could slice through them. The knots were too tight. She couldn't wiggle her wrists out of the loops.

Her gaze fell on a glass ashtray on a table behind her.

If she could break that . . . maybe she could use a sharp edge to cut the ropes binding her.

It was worth a shot.

Emmy didn't have many other options.

As the men faced off, Emmy leaned back in the chair. Her hands hit the ashtray and she tugged it.

It crashed on the floor.

Both men turned to her.

The man—Gilbert, Colby had called him— scowled and started to step toward her before stopping. "I don't know what you think you're doing . . . but it's not going to work."

Emmy only glared back at him.

Then her gaze turned to Colby.

Her Colby.

He would always be her Colby.

And he'd come to rescue her.

Emmy's life wouldn't be the same without him.

Would she have a chance to tell him that, though?

She didn't know.

Right now she needed to get the broken ashtray.

She had to slice through this rope, and she was running out of time.

Yet everything—*everything*—seemed to depend on it.

"YOU KNOW WHAT?" Gilbert muttered as he turned his resolve-filled gaze back onto Colby. "I think I'll take my chances."

Colby sucked in a breath.

He wasn't saying what Colby thought he was . . . or was he?

Before Colby could stop him, Gilbert lit the lighter and dropped it.

Flames whooshed across the floor.

As they did, the man sprinted toward the other side of the house.

Colby wanted to go stop him.

But he had to get to Emmy before the fire reached her.

Heat from the blaze already consumed the air as Colby dashed across the room.

Panic filled Emmy's eyes. "Colby . . . you've got to get out of here."

"Not without you." Colby tugged the ropes at her back.

Untying them was taking too long. Time wasn't on their side.

The fire was growing by the moment.

As Colby glanced at the flames, he made a split-second decision.

He lifted Emmy with the wooden chair still attached and flung her over his shoulder.

Then he darted toward the door.

There was still one path that led that way—a path without flames.

For now.

Smoke already filled the air. If he wasn't careful, it would invade their lungs. The inhalation alone would kill them.

He had no time to waste.

He raced toward the front of the house. The front door had been left open.

Gilbert must have escaped this way.

Colby only knew he wasn't going to let the woman he loved die.

He would sacrifice himself if he had to.

Doing otherwise wasn't even an option.

Finally, he reached the outdoors and gulped in a big breath of air.

They were almost to safety.

He carried Emmy down the stairs before setting her in front of him on the driveway. He then leaned toward her, desperate to see her eyes, to make sure she was truly okay.

"Emmy?" He gulped in more air.

Moisture pooled in her eyes as she nodded rapidly. "I'm fine, Colby. Thanks to you."

She opened her mouth as if she was about to say more.

But before any words left her lips, gunfire cracked the air.

Pain sliced through Colby.

He looked down and saw blood spreading across his chest.

"Colby?" Emmy gasped. "Colby!"

That's when he realized he'd been shot.

CHAPTER FIFTY-TWO

A SCREAM CAUGHT in Emmy's throat as she saw Colby sink to the ground. He'd been shot. No! No! *No!*

His staggered gaze locked on hers. "I love you, Emmy."

The air left her lungs at his proclamation.

"I love you too, Colby." As Emmy whispered the words, Colby's eyes closed.

He was losing consciousness, she realized.

A cry caught in her throat.

She desperately wanted to reach for him. To hold him up. To help him.

But she couldn't. She was a prisoner of this chair.

Just then, another gunshot rang through the air. Instinctively, Emmy stooped down.

Was that man still shooting? Hadn't he done enough damage?

Emmy glanced up, but the darkness prevented her from seeing any details.

If that man wanted to end her life, he could.

Shouts sounded in the distance. What was going on?

The next instant, Levi appeared in front of her.

His eyes lit with relief as he rushed toward her. But the look disappeared as his gaze traveled to Colby. Levi darted to him and knelt on the ground.

"The gunshot came out of nowhere." Emmy's voice cracked as emotion strangled her.

"He's still hanging in." Levi held two fingers to Colby's neck. "Are you okay, Emmy?"

"I'm fine. I'm just worried about Colby. Levi . . ." Her voice caught.

"Help is on the way."

"That gunman is still out there," Emmy said.

"Grant got him. The man is in custody. He's not going anywhere."

Relief filled her. At least there was that.

But this ordeal was far from over.

Colby . . .

Tears pooled in her eyes as she glanced at her best friend laying there lifelessly.

No . . . things couldn't end like this.

Sirens sounded in the distance.

Help was on the way, ready to take Colby to the hospital.

Emmy only prayed that they got there in time.

FOUR HOURS LATER, Emmy was allowed into Colby's room. He'd been life-flighted to a hospital in Norfolk, Virginia, the closest trauma center to Cape Corral.

Thankfully, Emmy had been allowed to go with him.

But the waiting had been agonizing.

Levi and the rest of the guys were still down in Cape Corral investigating. That was where they *should* be. They needed to find all the evidence they could before the elements washed any away.

But those hours of sitting by herself in the waiting room were beginning to wear on her. Emmy's thoughts had kept turning over and over.

She'd come so close to losing Colby. Too close.

She held back a whimper every time she thought about it.

Colby had been willing to sacrifice himself for

her. That was something that she would never, ever forget.

She pulled her chair as close to Colby's bed as she could and took his hand in hers.

His strong, calloused hand. One that had poked her in the side and pulled her hair and caught footballs.

The doctor said the bullet had missed any major organs—including his heart—but barely. Colby would need to stay in the hospital for a few days so doctors could monitor his status.

Things could have turned out a lot different.

Emmy was eternally grateful that Colby was still alive. That there was still a chance to make things right. To take a risk.

Outside, the nighttime had turned into daylight. As it did, Emmy rested her head on the edge of the bed and closed her eyes.

She loved Colby. She had no doubt about that.

Now he just needed to wake up so she could tell him that.

Emmy couldn't imagine her future without him. She was sorry it had taken something like today's events to make her realize that.

But now she never wanted to be away from her best friend again.

As she pressed her eyes closed, she lifted a prayer for Colby's recovery.

She also prayed that it wasn't too late for the two of them.

Emmy had already blown her chance once.

She wouldn't let that happen again. Not if she could help it.

CHAPTER FIFTY-THREE

AS COLBY'S eyes fluttered open, he heard a beeping sound in the distance.

His vision blurred, and everything appeared hazy around him.

He moaned as his head pounded.

Where was he? What had happened?

At once, memories flooded back to him.

Finding Emmy tied up in the house.

Gilbert holding the lighter.

The whole place going up in flames.

Then the gunshot.

Colby had been standing in front of Emmy when he'd felt the pain pierce his chest. Then everything had gone black.

Was Emmy okay? Had she been shot also?

Panic rushed through him. He blinked, desperate to see what was going on around him—desperate to know if Emmy was okay. Really okay.

The last thing Colby remembered was seeing the fear on her face.

Had that man shot her too?

Another groan from deep in his chest tried to escape—this one full of mourning and panic.

He tried to sit up. As he did, his heart pounded against his rib cage. But finally, his vision cleared.

He was in the hospital, he realized. His chest hurt something fierce. Numerous tubes were hooked up to him.

As he glanced down, he spotted Emmy. Her head rested at his bedside. Her arms were flung across his waist, and one hand held on to his.

His heart slowed.

Emmy was here.

With him.

And she was okay.

Joy burst inside him.

Thank You, God. Thank You, thank You, thank You!

As he muttered the silent prayer, Emmy lifted her head. Her gaze looked sleepy as she glanced around and there was a slight indentation on her face from where she'd rested her cheek against him.

Still, she had never looked more beautiful.

A smile feathered across her lips when she spotted Colby.

She straightened and squeezed his hand, the worry in her gaze turning to hope.

"Colby . . ." Her voice sounded scratchy with emotion as she studied him.

"You're okay." Colby's voice cracked as he said the words.

"I am. Thanks to you. If you hadn't gotten me out of that house when you did . . ." Her words trailed.

"I thought I was going to lose you." Colby's voice didn't even sound like his own. It was tight, and the words would hardly leave his lips as emotion clogged his throat.

"Oh, Colby . . ." More tears filled Emmy's eyes as she looked at him.

He squeezed her hand harder, wishing he could reach for her and pull her into an embrace. But the pain in his chest stopped him.

Emmy seemed to read the questions in his gaze —questions about what had happened after he blacked out.

"The bullet went in through your chest, but it missed any organs," she explained. "You're going to be sore for a while, but you're going to be okay."

"That's good to know, at least."

"It's very good to know." She smiled and wiped the moisture from her eyes using the edge of her sleeve.

Colby squeezed her hand again. "Don't cry. I'm still alive. It could be worse, right?"

Emmy let out a little laugh. "Yes, it could be." She paused and sniffled. "Colby . . ."

He held his breath, trying to anticipate whatever she might say next. "Yes?"

She shook her head and wiped beneath her eyes again as if her emotions were getting the best of her. "I just want you to know that . . . I love you."

Colby's heart pounded in his ears. Had he just heard correctly? And did Emmy mean she loved him as a friend? Or as something more? He didn't want to read too much into this.

"I love you too, Emmy."

She licked her lips, her expression seeming fragile with emotion. "When I thought I was going to lose you . . . I felt like my whole world crashed down. I can't stand the thought of you not being in my life."

His heart continued to pound in his chest as he listened to what Emmy had to say. He dared not interrupt. He needed to hear this. He *wanted* to hear this.

"Please, don't leave," she said. "I know it's selfish, and I don't want to be selfish. But my whole world on the island is wrapped up in you. Nothing would ever be the same if you left."

"So you want me to stay?" Colby repeated, just to make sure he had heard her correctly.

A smile curled her lips. "Yes, I want you to stay." Emmy lifted his hand and rested it against her cheek as she closed her eyes. "I want it to be you and me. Forever."

Warmth spread through him. Emmy did love him the way Colby loved her, didn't she? She'd felt the same spark when they had shared that kiss.

Joy burst inside him again.

Emmy stood and leaned toward him. Softly, she brushed her lips across his. "There will be more of that later—when I know that I'm not going to hurt you."

"I wouldn't really mind being hurt about now. I think the payoff would be worth it."

She chuckled. "You would say that."

Colby caught her hand as she tried to back away. "I love you too, Emmy Sutherland."

Her eyes misted with emotion. "I'm so glad to hear that."

Just then, the doctor walked in.

The two of them would have more time to talk later.

If things went according to Colby's plan, they'd have the rest of their lives.

And they'd give people on the island plenty to talk about.

THREE WEEKS LATER, Emmy was listening to "All I Want for Christmas Is You" and baking Christmas cookies for a friendly celebration that evening when she heard a knock on the door.

Before she could answer, someone stepped inside.

Colby.

A grin stretched across her face when she spotted him.

He was still recovering from the gunshot wound, but he was doing better. Until the doctor cleared him, Colby was on desk duty at the station. But he hoped that, in a few more weeks, he'd be back to active duty.

Emmy met him halfway across the room. As his arms circled her waist, Emmy rested her hands on

Colby's biceps. His chest was still sore, even though Colby would never admit it.

"I'm so glad you stopped by," she murmured.

"Of course. Every chance I have to see my girl." He winked.

"Or was it because you could smell the Christmas cookies over at the station?"

He shrugged. "That too."

She giggled as Colby winked at her.

Instead of stepping back and offering him a snickerdoodle, Emmy reached on her tiptoes and planted a soft kiss on his lips.

It was one of many they'd exchanged since Colby had come home from the hospital.

In fact, Emmy had set him up in one of her upstairs rooms so she could take care of him.

She'd enjoyed every moment of being his nurse, despite the way Colby had playfully complained every chance he had.

Emmy had feared things might turn awkward between the two of them once their heightened emotions wore off. But awkwardness was nowhere to be found. In fact, Emmy felt happier than ever.

She started to step back when Colby pulled her even closer.

"You taste like a snickerdoodle," he murmured, his gaze smoky with emotion.

"I may have sampled a few cookies."

"Let me double check that taste one more time." He leaned toward her and his mouth captured hers.

Emmy didn't complain. If she wasn't careful, she would let herself get caught up in this moment and her guests tonight would have nothing to eat.

Finally, she forced herself to step back. Her heart still raced as she stared up at her best friend. "I do need to pull some cookies out of the oven."

She tapped her palm against his shoulder, tempted to stay right here.

"Do you have to?" Colby attempted to pull her closer again, but Emmy slipped away from his touch.

"Only if I don't want my cookies to burn. My favorite firefighter isn't available right now to put out any blazes at this house."

"I'd say there's a pretty great fire between us right now."

Emmy playfully poked his arm. "You're just full of those awful one-liners, aren't you?"

He shrugged, his eyes still glimmering with humor. "I try."

"Come on in the kitchen. Let me get these cookies."

As Emmy pulled the tray from the oven, she let out a contented sigh.

Things finally felt fairly normal.

Luther was dead. His greedy motives would never hurt anyone again. Though Emmy didn't wish death on him, his actions had hurt a lot of people—and ultimately, his actions had hurt him.

Gilbert—whose real name was John Allister—was in jail. The truth had come out when Levi interrogated him.

It turned out that John had followed Luther to the island, trying to get the money Luther owed him because of gambling debts. While there, John had encountered Jeremy Riesling, realized he was a part of Luther's scheme, and he'd tried to get information out of him.

When Jeremy had shared that he'd come to the island looking for treasure left by his ancestors, John had beaten him trying to get more details. Jeremy managed to escape and call 911, but his connection was spotty.

In that time, John had found Jeremy, gotten the information he needed, and then shot him.

Colby's dad would go on trial for arson soon. He faced a possible twelve years in prison. Though Colby said he had mixed feelings on the issue, Mr.

Morris seemed content to do time for his crimes. He still claimed the arsons were "righteous" and that people would one day realize he was a hero.

Despite those things, hope was on the horizon. If only the locals could fix the situation with the Fergusons, then everything would be golden.

Speaking of golden . . . that gold that had been found was the real deal. It was worth nearly a million dollars.

Officials were searching now for the rightful owner. Last Emmy had heard, they hadn't found any relatives to claim it. Emmy had a feeling those people were out there, and, once they heard the news, there would probably be lots of fighting over who got what.

She wouldn't wish that kind of stress on anyone.

Emmy didn't have that much money, but she had enough. That kind of cash didn't make a person happy—being around the people you loved did.

She planned on enjoying this Christmas on the island, surrounded by her favorite people in the whole world.

She leaned toward the warm pan of cookies, relishing in the scents of cinnamon and sugar that filled the air. When she turned back toward Colby, he held something in his hands . . . while down on one knee.

Emmy gasped as she stared at the object, uncertain if she were seeing things correctly.

But she was.

He held an engagement ring.

Her gaze darted to Colby's. "What . . . ?"

"I wanted to wait until Christmas, but I can't." Colby held up the ring. "Emmy Sue Sutherland, you've made me the happiest guy alive. You're my best friend, my soul mate, and the one I want to spend forever with. I've known it for nearly twenty years, but I'm tired of waiting. Will you marry me?"

She didn't have to think about her answer. "I would be honored to marry you, Colby Morris."

As Emmy extended her hand, Colby slipped the ring onto her finger. She looked at the princess-cut diamond only for a moment before looking back at Colby. Tears of happiness streamed from her eyes.

She flung her arms around him and their lips met.

Emmy looked forward to doing this for the rest of her life . . . with the man who was her best friend and the love of her life.

~~~
~~~

Thank you so much for reading *Seagrass Secrets*. If you enjoyed this book, I would love for you to leave a review! Reviews are a huge help for authors.

Stay tuned for *Driftwood Danger* coming soon!

To keep up with all the latest news, sign up for my newsletter at: www.christybarritt.com.

#13 Cold Case: Clean Getaway

#14 Cold Case: Clean Sweep

#15 Cold Case: Clean Break

#16 Cleans to an End (coming soon)

While You Were Sweeping, A Riley Thomas Spinoff

The Sierra Files:

#1 Pounced

#2 Hunted

#3 Pranced

#4 Rattled

The Gabby St. Claire Diaries (a Tween Mystery series):

The Curtain Call Caper

The Disappearing Dog Dilemma

The Bungled Bike Burglaries

The Worst Detective Ever

#1 Ready to Fumble

#2 Reign of Error

#3 Safety in Blunders

#4 Join the Flub

#5 Blooper Freak

#6 Flaw Abiding Citizen

#7 Gaffe Out Loud

#8 Joke and Dagger

#9 Wreck the Halls

#10 Glitch and Famous (coming soon)

Raven Remington

Relentless 1

Relentless 2 (coming soon)

Holly Anna Paladin Mysteries:

#1 Random Acts of Murder

#2 Random Acts of Deceit

#2.5 Random Acts of Scrooge

#3 Random Acts of Malice

#4 Random Acts of Greed

#5 Random Acts of Fraud

#6 Random Acts of Outrage

#7 Random Acts of Iniquity

Lantern Beach Mysteries

#1 Hidden Currents

#2 Flood Watch

#3 Storm Surge

#4 Dangerous Waters

#5 Perilous Riptide

#6 Deadly Undertow

Lantern Beach Romantic Suspense

Tides of Deception

Shadow of Intrigue

Storm of Doubt

Winds of Danger

Rains of Remorse

Torrents of Fear

Lantern Beach P.D.

On the Lookout

Attempt to Locate

First Degree Murder

Dead on Arrival

Plan of Action

Lantern Beach Escape

Afterglow (a novelette)

Lantern Beach Blackout

Dark Water

Safe Harbor

Ripple Effect

Rising Tide

Crime á la Mode

Deadman's Float

Milkshake Up

Bomb Pop Threat

Banana Split Personalities

The Sidekick's Survival Guide

The Art of Eavesdropping

The Perks of Meddling

The Exercise of Interfering

The Practice of Prying

The Skill of Snooping

The Craft of Being Covert

Saltwater Cowboys

Saltwater Cowboy

Breakwater Protector

Cape Corral Keeper

Seagrass Secrets

Driftwood Danger (coming soon)

Carolina Moon Series

Home Before Dark

Gone By Dark

Wait Until Dark

Light the Dark

Taken By Dark

Suburban Sleuth Mysteries:

Death of the Couch Potato's Wife

Fog Lake Suspense:

Edge of Peril

Margin of Error

Brink of Danger

Line of Duty

Cape Thomas Series:

Dubiosity

Disillusioned

Distorted

Standalone Romantic Mystery:

The Good Girl

Suspense:

Imperfect

The Wrecking

Sweet Christmas Novella:

Home to Chestnut Grove

Standalone Romantic-Suspense:

Keeping Guard

The Last Target

Race Against Time

Ricochet

Key Witness

Lifeline

High-Stakes Holiday Reunion

Desperate Measures

Hidden Agenda

Mountain Hideaway

Dark Harbor

Shadow of Suspicion

The Baby Assignment

The Cradle Conspiracy

Trained to Defend

Mountain Survival (coming soon)

Nonfiction:

Characters in the Kitchen

Changed: True Stories of Finding God through Christian Music (out of print)

The Novel in Me: The Beginner's Guide to Writing and Publishing a Novel (out of print)

ABOUT THE AUTHOR

USA Today has called Christy Barritt's books "scary, funny, passionate, and quirky."

Christy writes both mystery and romantic suspense novels that are clean with underlying messages of faith. Her books have won the Daphne du Maurier Award for Excellence in Suspense and Mystery, have been twice nominated for the Romantic Times Reviewers' Choice Award, and have finaled for both a Carol Award and Foreword Magazine's Book of the Year.

She is married to her Prince Charming, a man who thinks she's hilarious—but only when she's not trying to be. Christy is a self-proclaimed klutz, an avid music lover who's known for spontaneously bursting into song, and a road trip aficionado.

When she's not working or spending time with her family, she enjoys singing, playing the guitar, and exploring small, unsuspecting towns where people have no idea how accident-prone she is.

Find Christy online at:
www.christybarritt.com
www.facebook.com/christybarritt
www.twitter.com/cbarritt

Sign up for Christy's newsletter to get information on all of her latest releases here: www.christybarritt.com/newsletter-sign-up/

If you enjoyed this book, please consider leaving a review.

www.ingramcontent.com/pod-product-compliance
Lightning Source LLC
Chambersburg PA
CBHW031438160726
47994CB00005B/1784